CURTIS
THE HUNTER SERIES BOOK 2

KATHI S. BARTON

This is a work of fiction. Names, characters, places, and incidents are products of the author's imagination or are used fictitiously and are not to be construed as real. Any resemblance to actual events, locations, organizations, or persons, living or dead, is entirely coincidental.

World Castle Publishing, LLC
Pensacola, Florida
Copyright © Kathi S. Barton 2013
Paperback ISBN: 9781938961861
eBook ISBN: 9781938961878
First Edition World Castle Publishing, LLC, February 1, 2013
http://www.worldcastlepublishing.com
Licensing Notes
All rights reserved. No part of this book may be used or reproduced in any manner whatsoever without written permission, except in the case of brief quotations embodied in articles and reviews.
Cover: Karen Fuller
Editor: Brieanna Robertson

Chapter 1

She was late. He wasn't really surprised, but it did annoy him. He looked at his watch again and wondered just how much longer he was supposed to wait before it would be considered bad form if he left. Probably should give her more than ten minutes. But he wasn't giving her much more than thirty. He had things to do. And none of them had anything to do with waiting on a woman who was forever late.

Curtis hadn't wanted to come to this meeting, but his brother Daniel had begged off by saying that he had to be in court. Curtis was pretty sure he'd been had, that nothing more pressing than not being here with Kylie was all it was. She'd been a thorn in his side since they'd been kids.

Kylie had hung on Daniel's every word. And as far as she was concerned, there was nothing he couldn't do or say that she didn't believe. And Daniel had used the girl mercilessly by having her do his homework and chores every chance he'd gotten. That is until he'd found Meghan Steele and her boobs when he'd been fifteen.

Curtis ordered a salad, thinking that he'd better do something in the event the girl didn't show. He grinned at the waitress when she winked at him but sobered quickly when he saw his mother coming toward him. He stood when she approached the table and pulled out her chair when she moved toward it.

"I didn't think I was going to make it." She ordered a small salad and a glass of tea and turned to the empty seat. "Is she in the ladies' room?"

"No. Late. I just ordered a salad because I can't wait much longer. I have a meeting with some of the people who are helping Kasey with her training on the new system. She's going to be a heck of an addition to our security team." He nodded when his mom ordered a salad too. "I was trying to remember when the last time we saw her was. Kylie, I mean. She must have been about seventeen or so."

"I think you might be right. Her father said she toured Europe for about two years while she worked at different papers there. Then when she'd settled down in France, she'd landed a good job at one of the bigger papers and worked her way through her Masters in Journalism. Jon is very proud of her."

He wouldn't have thought the girl had that much spine but said nothing. When the owner of the restaurant came toward them, he was sure it was to tell them that Kylie wasn't coming and that she'd meet them later. He was stunned when he pulled out a chair, and this…vision sat down.

"I'm sorry I'm late. I overslept." She smiled at his mother. "Hello, Mrs. Hunter. It's been a very long time. How is your family?"

"Kylie?" The girl nodded and glanced at him. He could tell she was upset or nervous. Maybe both. "My goodness, look at you. I wouldn't have recognized you for any amount of money. Curtis, say something."

He didn't, couldn't. He could only stare at her and think that he was very happy with his brother right now and hoped that he'd be able to repay him. Finally, when she cocked a lovely brow at him, he cleared his throat. "I'm sorry. Like my mother, I didn't recognize you. You've grown into a very beautiful woman." He smiled when she flushed. "I didn't mean to embarrass you."

"It's nothing." She looked around. "Is Daniel coming? I thought he and I were going to meet. Is he running behind as well?"

"He's not coming," Curtis said quickly, then flushed when his mother gave him an odd look. "What I mean is, he's tied up in court. He sends his apologies."

Curtis thought he heard Kylie say something like, "I bet he did," but didn't get a chance to ask when the waiter took that moment to come and ask if they were ready to order. He also set his mother's salad and his in front of them.

"Oh my, look at this." Curtis looked at his mother, who had a small book in her hand. "I have to be at the library right now. I completely forgot about it." She turned to the waiter and asked him if he could please box up her salad. He took off to do her bidding.

"Mom, you said you cleared your day to be here with Kylie so that we could get those articles taken care of as well as a couple of other things." He both wanted to see her stay and also have her go. But he couldn't let go of the look on Kylie's face when she'd heard that Daniel wasn't coming.

"I forgot." She stood up, and he did as well. "No, no. You two can iron this out. I have to go. Thank you, dear, for coming here, and please call, and we'll have to get together for lunch again. When I'm not so busy."

Then she was gone. Curtis looked at Kylie, who was

suddenly very interested in her menu. He didn't know why that pissed him off, but it did. She wanted Daniel, and Curtis would never stand in the way if he wanted her too. "You don't have to stay. I can have my brother call your office and set something more up if—"

"We both know that he no more wants to be here than you do." When he started to answer her, she leaned down and picked up a steno pad. "Let's just get this finished, shall we? I'm sure you have plenty to do other than sit with a childhood pest and try to make small talk."

He realized she was mad. He had no idea why that made him want to laugh, but he was smart enough to know to keep his laughter to himself. But before he could comment, his phone rang. While he answered his brother's call, she pulled out a small recorder, as well as a very feminine pen.

"Well?" Daniel asked. Curtis knew what he was asking him, but didn't want to answer his question.

"Well, what?" A pause at the other end had him chuckle, and he looked into Kylie's eyes when she looked at him. He decided that green was his favorite eye color.

"Well, is she still a rolly polly kid in braces? Or has she gotten fatter? Christ, you don't think that is possible, do you? She was nearly as big as a house then."

"You'd be incorrect in that assumption." Curtis hoped his brother was smart enough to know that he'd not be able to answer him, and he confirmed it with his next question.

"She's right next to you, isn't she? Shit. Curtis, please tell me she's not a raving beauty and that I'm a sucker for not going to the meeting with her?" His pleading voice had him smile. Then he looked at her.

They all knew that Kylie had been lovesick over their brother. It had been the source of many fights when they'd sang the *k-i-s-s-i-n-g* song as boys. Now, though, they were all grown up, and Curtis wanted to see if she kissed as well as he thought she might.

"Of course. You can speak to her yourself." He handed out his phone to her. He could hear his brother yelling at the other end. "It's Daniel. He'd like to speak to you."

She put the phone to her ear and smiled at him. "He seems to think you are going to die an untimely death soon and that he'll be going to prison for a very long time."

"I can take him." Curtis ordered for them when the waiter returned. Kylie spoke to Daniel and pointed to what she wanted. Nothing small and girlish about her appetite, and he found himself envious of his brother.

~~~

Kylie's heart fluttered when she heard his voice. It had been at least a decade since she'd heard it, and even him being obviously pissed at his brother made her think of him in the nicest way. But she kept glancing over at the man beside her and nearly missed what Daniel was saying to her.

"...tomorrow night if you want. I can get out of the fundraiser with my family, and we can go and have a nice quiet dinner and get reacquainted. I can pick you up at your place and—"

"I'm sorry, but if you mean the charity thing tomorrow night, I'm already going. Our firm is making a donation, and my father is going to give a speech. You can meet me there if you'd like."

She wanted to do just as he'd asked her to. Alone with the one man she'd spent nearly all her life wanting to marry. She was beyond that now, but to be seen with him, be with him, she would have done just about anything. With the exception of disappointing her dad. Not even for Daniel.

"I'll have a date with me, but she'll understand about old friends." She knew that it would to her no matter who she was and how old of friends they were. "I'll see you there then. Can I please speak to my brother?"

Kylie handed the phone to him and dug into her salad. She heard him say a few things, nothing that she understood, but it didn't matter to her. She was going to be seeing Daniel tomorrow night. And the dress she had would be perfect. She looked up at her lunch companion when she heard the phone close.

"He said to tell you thanks." His voice had gone from gentle and nice before the call to now sounding hard and a little pissed. As he ate his own salad, she tried to think about what she'd done. When nothing was forthcoming, she asked him.

"Nothing." That didn't sound any better, but before she could ask again, he continued. "I'd like to set up a series of articles about the thing that happened with my sister-in-law a few months back. It's been settled, but I want to make sure that other firms aren't having the same thing happening under their noses. She and some others that worked for us were abused. I'm not at liberty to say much, only to say how they were hurt, and they were taken advantage of by one of our employees."

"So we're talking PR. Okay, I can make you look as good as you think you need to. I would suggest that you—"

"I don't want you to make us look good. I want you to paint the picture just how it happened. I want you to tell your readers that we screwed up. That we had a problem and we didn't take care of it until it was nearly too late. I want it to be about how we didn't know, but that didn't make us any less guilty."

She glared at him after their lunch was served, and their salad plates are taken away. "You want me to 'paint,' as you called it, that you're the poor victim in all this, and everyone should feel sorry for you?" She could tell he was pissed at her, but she was getting just as pissed at him. "Oh wait, you want me to make it sound as if you'd been taken advantage of and that the only way you'll feel better is if someone comes and buys whatever it is you're selling."

When he leaned back in his chair and glared, she thought maybe she'd pushed back a little too hard. Damn it. He'd started this. But her dad had told her that she was to do whatever they needed, that the Hunters could mean the difference between their company surviving for a few more years or not. Her dad had just figured out that no one was reading papers anymore and wanted it online or on their phone. She had to smile at his assumption that the paper would be fine. Not without being a little more modern, it wouldn't, and she was going to work on that as soon as he'd let her.

"Do you always come across as a bitch when trying to drum up business, or is it because I'm not your precious Daniel?" Curtis stood. "I think you'll write what you want and, frankly, I'm not sure I care what you do. But you write anything other than what I want, and I'll own that failing paper of your father's as well as all the property he's mortgaged to keep it going."

He left her sitting there with her fork halfway to her mouth. She looked around to see if anyone else had heard their exchange, and it seemed that everyone was enjoying their own meal. She laid her fork down and closed her eyes. She'd fucked up royally.

Her dad had told her that they needed this account to make other firms see that the Hunters were still using paper.

And apparently, Curtis knew that as well. Their paper wasn't going to fail, not if she had anything to do with it. She told her dad she would help him, and she would. She knew that if he knew what she'd done, he'd be disappointed in her. Well, she was too.

"We didn't change when everyone else did like you said we should. We did put a little effort into it, but now…who would have thought that the changes in the way people read papers would have come about so quickly?" She had told him to get with it but said nothing as he poured his heart out to her. "I should have listened to you and the others. But I'm a stubborn fool, stubborn old fool. And now look at us. Not doing all that well, and we're only halfway through the year."

She'd been shocked by that. Staggered really, and he was counting on her to make this one thing work. She knew at times he could be a little pessimistic, and she knew that if given a chance to see the books, things would be much better than he'd said. He hoped that with Hunters running ads, others would as well, and that would help them make the transition from paper to web.

Kylie was suddenly not hungry. When the waiter came to refill her water glass, she asked for the bill.

"Mr. Hunter took care of it, miss. He said that something came up and that he'd had to leave early, but I was to make sure you had everything you needed." He looked so eager to do just that, and she knew that Curtis had tipped him very well. "Can I get you anything else? We have some nice desserts if you'd like."

"No, thank you. I have a sudden headache." And belly too, if she was honest with him. Picking up her purse, she asked him if she could please have her lunch removed and took out her cell. "I'll be gone shortly."

He told her to take her time and walked away with hers and Curtis' plates. She dialed the number she'd called only this morning to confirm the appointment. Someone answered on the first ring.

"Yes, I'd like to make an appointment with Curtis Hunter, please. Today, if possible." The girl asked her to hold on.

"I'm sorry, ma'am, but he's cleared his appointments today for a luncheon meeting. I can call him and ask if he'll be finished soon and call you back." So he'd cleared his calendar for her. Now she felt doubly stupid. "Would you like that?"

"Yes, please. Tell him that it's Kylie Washington. And that I'd really like to speak to him as soon as possible."

The girl hesitated for a few seconds before she said what Kylie thought she would. "His day was cleared for you, Miss Washington. Did he not make the appointment? I'll ask his mother, but she too cleared her calendar for this meeting."

No library meeting either. Kylie wondered what she was up to, but told the girl that she had had to give him information and she had it now. She crossed her fingers when she was put on hold.

"Miss Washington, Mr. Hunter said that if you could be here in thirty minutes and not be late, then he'll see you." The girl, like the man, sounded colder, and she could only imagine what Curtis had said to her.

"I'll be there." She gathered her things as soon as she closed her phone. This might be her only chance to help her dad, and she wasn't going to fuck it up twice in one day. She'd be courteous as well as polite, and she'd make this work even if it killed her. And maybe if she was really good, she'd get to see Daniel.

She arrived with one minute to spare but didn't count on having to be badged into the impressive building. After checking her identification that she'd had to go back out to her car and get and then calling to see if she indeed had an appointment, she was sitting in his front lobby twenty-five minutes later. She was still fuming about the wait when Curtis came out of his office.

"You're late." He made a point of looking at his watch. "I said thirty minutes, and you're at nearly an hour. Do you make a habit of making appointments you don't intend to be on time for?"

She looked at his secretary and noticed that she stared at him as well. Furious and embarrassed, she stood up and put her purse on her arm. Nothing was important enough to be treated this way. She didn't say a word as she made her way to the elevator. Pushing the button to go down, she pulled out her cell phone. "Daddy, it's me. I won't be able to do this. I'm coming home." The elevator opened, and she stepped in. Just as the doors were coming to a close, she saw Curtis coming toward her. She didn't move, and when the doors snapped closed, she let go of the breath she didn't know she'd been holding.

She lost the signal. And wiping at the tears that were surely smearing her makeup, she put her phone away. The nerve of the man treating her that way. She wasn't stupid, and if he'd simply listened to her, she could have explained that she'd been made late because of him. She had hoped she could make a good impression on him, and all she'd managed to do was to make her daddy's firm look incompetent.

The elevator opened, and she was nearly halfway across the lobby when a guard was suddenly in front of her. She tried to step around him, first to the left, then right, and he simply smiled at her.

"He called you, right?" He nodded. "I don't want to see

him. Does that make a difference?"

"No, ma'am. He said you were to be brought back up to his office, and he didn't sound all that happy about you either if you want to know the truth." He nodded to the elevator that she'd just come out of. "You ready?"

She looked at his name tag and saw that his name was Officer York. She'd read somewhere that Royce had married a York and wondered if this man was related. She moved to the right again, hoping he'd let her go. In the end, she moved toward what she'd come to think of as her ride to hell. "Officer York, I don't suppose I could persuade you to let me go and to tell him you didn't catch me?" He nodded to the cameras over their head. "I see. He knows all and sees all. Bastard."

The officer looked at her with a raised brow, and she hastened to explain she'd meant his boss and not him.

"He's my niece's brother-in-law. I like Curtis, a great deal as a matter of fact." He stepped in the small box with her. She noticed he also had his hand on his gun. "But I'm pretty sure his parents were married when he was born. Can't know that for sure, but there you have it."

She didn't answer. She was too mad to appreciate him trying to calm her with his good old boy humor. She looked at the seam in the door and wondered if, when they opened, she could make it to the stairs before he came to get her again. She saw that her makeup was indeed smeared when she saw her reflection and thought *fuck it*. He'd made her come back, and she certainly wasn't going to make an effort to *gussy up*, as her grandmother used to say.

When the elevator opened, he was standing there. And he didn't look the least bit pissed. In fact, she would say that he looked quite pleased with himself. When he waved his hand toward where he'd come from earlier, she walked past him and into the office.

She was not going to do business with him even if she had to work at a fast food restaurant to get the extra money her dad needed to make the change-over. Curtis Hunter was not a thing like his brother.

Chapter 2

Daniel stood when his brother and a gorgeous woman walked in. When Curtis had asked him to come into his office and wait, he'd had no idea what was going on. The woman, even in her obvious anger, looked good enough to eat.

"Daniel," Curtis started. "You remember Kylie. Kylie is a bit pissed at me, and I thought you might like to help me calm her a bit."

"You prick." The softly spoken words caught him off guard, and Daniel looked at Curtis, who was laughing hard. "You know…damn you to hell."

"Probably, but this concerns the welfare of a company, and I'll not have a kid with her panties in a twist fuck it up for the rest of us. Sit." Curtis went behind his desk as if he truly expected her to sit. She moved toward the door instead.

He looked between the two of them and decided that, while he had no idea what was going on, it looked like it might be fun. Besides, who didn't want to be around a very beautiful woman who had made his usually unflappable brother so angry? He sat when Curtis stopped Kylie and brought her back to the chair.

"I said, sit."

She sat but perched herself on the edge of the chair so that he knew as well as, he suspected, his brother did that she wasn't going to remain there for long.

"You made this appointment now tell me what you wanted."

"Nothing." She stood, and so did Curtis. Daniel nearly lost control of his humor when she glared at Curtis as she sat again. This was proving to be much more fun than he'd had in months. "I've decided that in no way do I want to do business with you. You're an...you're an arrogant ass, and I've never been so mistreated in my life."

Curtis snorted. "I'll just bet your pampered little ass hasn't had a sharp word said to you since you came out with that silver spoon in your mouth." When she stood again, so did Curtis. "You need my business, or you go under. It's as simple as that."

"I'd rather live in my car."

Daniel stood when she spoke again. Okay, this wasn't so funny anymore. He knew that the paper was having issues, but not that bad.

Curtis looked at him. "You need to step out, please. I need to have a word with her." The sharp jerk of his thumb pointed at Kylie. When Daniel started to protest, Curtis spoke again. "I won't hurt her no matter how tempting it is."

Daniel looked at the two of them nearly standing toe to toe, well, as close as they could get with a desk between them. He had an idea that when these two came together, there was going to be either a great deal of blood or fireworks. Right now, he was betting on the blood. Nodding once to them both he went to the door and opened it. Turning back, he looked at them.

"I'll be right outside if you need me. Just…just scream." Daniel was sure that neither of them heard him. His brother was coming around his desk when he closed the door.

Harriet was sitting behind her desk when he came out. She was a lovely little thing, and he'd been flirting with her for months. He wasn't allowed to date her, which he supposed was fine in all, but he did think they could have some fun here. Before he could settle on her desk and begin what he called fun-play, the door to Curtis' office opened, and he stormed out.

"You deal with her." The file slapped him in the chest. "I can't…she's the most…I'm not going to be around her very…" Curtis took a deep breath, and that's when Daniel noticed the brightening handprint on his cheek. Christ, she'd hit him. "There's all you need. Make her see reason. I'm going out."

Daniel watched his brother move to the elevators and, when it opened and closed after he stepped into it, Curtis looked at Harriet. She shrugged and smiled. This was too weird. Taking the file, he entered the office.

He had no idea what he expected, but Kylie standing near Curtis' desk wasn't it. She wasn't moving. He wasn't sure she was even breathing. When he walked up to her and touched her shoulder, she looked at him as if she'd never seen him before. Then promptly burst into tears.

Daniel was going to murder his brother. Taking the obviously distressed woman into his arms, he held her as she cried. Daniel was thinking of ways to make Curtis suffer and decided that telling their mom would have the most effect. She would make him hurt in more ways than he ever could. He realized while he'd been plotting against his brother Kylie was simply holding him, and she'd stopped crying. Daniel lifted her chin up and looked into her tear-stained face.

"He kissed me."

To say he was shocked by her statement would have been a major understatement.

"He came around that big desk and yanked me to him and kissed me."

"I see." He didn't, but she seemed to think that was fine. "Did he say…did he say why he kissed you?" Sounded reasonable to him.

"No. He's so…did you know that he yelled at me in the restaurant? Talked to me like I was ten or something. I'm not ten years old anymore, and I won't have him treating me so." Her body pressed against his had him agreeing that she wasn't ten, not by a long shot. "And to tell me I had thirty minutes to get here and then to have to give my signature, nearly in blood, before they'd let me come up here…I was late because he is so untrusting."

It took him a few seconds to think about what she meant and realized it was the security team. He didn't think that pointing out they'd had some issues recently, as well as them being nearly all in-house, would be a good thing right now. Now, he thought, was not the time. He wondered what had made Curtis, a normally calm, cool, and collected guy who never got upset no matter what, let a little thing like Kylie piss him off.

But he intended to find out.

~~~

Curtis ran as fast as the treadmill would go. He felt the sweat run down his back in rivers, and even his legs were sweating. He watched the monitor in front of him without seeing it. The woman in his office was the only thing on his mind. And the kiss.

Christ, what had he been thinking? He was mad, sure, but to kiss her like that was...his family, hell, his mother was going to kill him. He'd been raised to never take advantage of someone smaller, younger, especially not a woman. He was dead meat.

"You okay, C?"

Curtis looked over at the blond, Linda he thought her name was, who worked here. "You're running there like it's life or death. I'd very much like it if you'd slow it down a bit and take a water break. Not having you code out on my shift."

He didn't stop or slow it down. He owned this fucking place, and if he wanted to run until his feet fell off and he bled to death, then he'd damn well do it. When she reached over and lowered the speed, he found himself wanting to snarl. Before he could do anything, he glanced at his reflection in the now blackened screen.

He looked...well, he looked insane. Maybe even was for what he'd been doing and what he'd done. He slowed the treadmill until he was walking and not running. Linda walked away and went to harass someone else. He'd come straight here from his office. It was that or go back to his office, press Kylie against the closest hard surface, and fuck her until he had her out of his system. But he couldn't. He wouldn't. She was and had been in love with Daniel since they were kids.

She'd been a pest to them all. Daniel would use her, he'd have her do his homework even though he already had it done. He would tease her until she blushed while the rest of them would simply ignore her. He remembered the first time she'd been allowed to hang out with them.

He'd been sixteen, and Daniel had been just a little over two years younger. Daniel was already showing signs of being a flirt and was pretty good at it. Curtis would watch him get girl after girl while he usually stayed home on Friday nights. Curtis had always been overly shy, and it had taken him years to work through it enough that he could go out. He'd gotten better at it, or the women bolder, as he and his family started making money, and now he had dates even when he didn't want them.

But Kylie had always been different. She had been in puppy love with Daniel at twelve. She would watch them, especially him, from her perch on the porch of her father's house. They already had all the money as far as the Hunters, who didn't have two nickels to rub together but were going somewhere fast. Then they'd been a man short for some football play.

He grimaced when he remembered her trying her best to figure out the calls and when she'd been handed the ball by Daniel, she'd frozen. He'd tried his best to stop, but his feet, too big for his growing body, hadn't been all that helpful. Curtis had hit her full tilt and took them both to the ground. When he managed to roll off her, she was unconscious, bloodied, and still holding onto the stupid ball.

He'd been grounded for a week. His mother had lectured him for an hour, then his father had come into his room and sat on his bed. He didn't say anything for a long while, simply sat, and stared at the wall across from them. And when he did speak, Curtis had been so grateful and so relieved that he'd never forgotten it.

"Girls want more than they should have. I'm not talking about jobs, mind you. Some of the women I work with should be in charge instead of the idiots that are there now. No, I'm talking about playing." He stopped talking, and Curtis looked at him.

"Playing? You mean sex?" His dad looked at him and

smiled, and Curtis knew that's not what he meant. "You mean football?"

"Yes, sometimes. It could be a girl might think she's built for it; some are, but there are ones that simply want to do it because someone told them they couldn't. Like little Kylie. Her daddy doesn't let her run wild like you boys do. Probably thinks he's protecting her, but he's only hurting her. Maybe she'll figure it out, maybe not." He looked at him. "You understand what I'm saying?"

Curtis thought about it. Did he? He wasn't sure, but he was going to try his best. "She wants to play with us because her daddy told her she couldn't. She doesn't even care that she can't do it well, she just wants to…to prove that she can."

His dad laughed. "Something like that. Like your grades. Remember how that teacher told your mom and me you'd never amount to much because you had your head in the clouds? What did I tell you then?"

"That I could do whatever I wanted so long as I did it with honesty and with all my heart." Curtis looked at his dad as he continued. "You're saying that she's been told she's a girl and needs to stay on her porch and wait for some boy to come along and care for her. But she doesn't like it any better than we would."

His dad had stood up and ruffled his hair. "Kylie Washington isn't always going to have everything handed to her. Someday, someone is going to have to come along and show her how to survive. But as Hunters, we can give her a few lessons now to prepare her. Curtis, you were playing. So was she. If she got hurt, it was not only your fault but hers as well. But more her daddy's. You owned up to what you'd done, got her care, and even stayed with her until someone took her to the hospital. I'm proud of you, son."

He'd walked out of his room, and Curtis went to his desk. He pulled out his application to Yale and studied it. He was graduating from high school in twenty-three days and then to college. He'd only had three weeks to make a boy out of her.

Curtis was in the shower when his brother said his name. He'd come in there when he was sure it was empty and simply wanted to be left alone with his memories. He'd been cruel to Kylie. Not that he regretted kissing her, but—

"What the hell is wrong with you?"

He looked over at Daniel, who was standing just outside the showers in his suit and tie.

"She said you kissed her."

Curtis turned off the shower and grabbed his towel. "You can tell her it won't happen again. Did you get her to go over those proposals I made up?" Curtis hoped he'd go away when he went to his locker, but when he came out of the changing room, he was still there. Curtis tried to ignore him.

"You were in charge of the paper. Mom said you were the best at getting the point across without being a hothead." Daniel snorted. "I would have normally thought so too, but after this morning, I'm not so sure."

He agreed with him silently and continued to dress. But apparently, Daniel wasn't going to be put off nor, it seemed, was he going to do as he'd asked him and get her to sign off on the proposals.

"She's going to talk with us tomorrow night at the ball. You'd better be nice to her or Mom will hear about how you made her cry." Curtis started to say something nasty to his brother but was stopped when he raised his hand. "I mean it, Curtis. I like this girl, and I won't have you messing it up for me."

And that, as they say, was that. He nodded once and

grabbed up his jacket. He stared at Daniel for several seconds before he put out his hand. "Congratulations. I wish you all the best." *Like hell*, he thought. But he wouldn't do anything, not all the things he'd been imagining doing with her, to her since she'd come across the restaurant in that little skirt and oh so lovely blouse. No, Curtis would never encroach on his brother's women. No matter how much he wanted to.

His phone was ringing when he entered his office. He nearly didn't answer it but picked it up anyway. Harriet was already gone and, apparently, had forgotten to put the calls to the service again. Curtis needed someone to replace her but was too sure that in her family, she was the only one working, and it wouldn't go well for them.

"I thought I'd get…I need to make an appointment with you. I have tomorrow open and then Monday. After that, I have other things I have to do."

Curtis closed his eyes to Kylie's voice. He didn't need this. "I turned the whole thing over to Daniel. He's the one you'll be meeting with from now on." He opened the calendar on the shared drive that they all added to. "He can meet with you Monday morning at eight." He didn't point out that he was busy after ten and that she needed to be on time for this one. She was no longer his problem. He waited for her to answer with his fingers curved over the keys.

"All right. I have everything in my possession, including the file."

He keyed in the time and with whom, hoping she'd just hang up.

"Why?"

He stopped typing and waited for more. When nothing was forthcoming, he leaned back in his chair after saving the entry. He knew what she was asking him, but didn't want to deal with it. Or why he'd done it. "Because I have other commitments that have cropped up. I have a large firm I'm purchasing in a few days that needs my utmost—"

"That's not what I meant, and you damn well know it. Why did you kiss me? Especially being so angry?"

She had claws. He liked that. She'd need them if Daniel and she were to become a couple. Daniel hadn't been a one woman man since he'd been a kid. He frowned when he still didn't have an answer.

"I won't allow it to happen again." He sat up in his chair, suddenly too tired to cope with her. "If you have any more questions, please refer them to Daniel. He'll work with you from now on." He put the phone in the cradle then stood. He sat back down, ignored the ringing phone, and pressed another button. After putting the phones to go to the service, he left. It was going to be a long night.

Chapter 3

Kylie called her dad. He wouldn't help her, she knew. One, because she wasn't going to tell him why she didn't want to go tonight. And secondly, she couldn't go tonight no matter what. If she had to see even one of the Hunter men, she might not be able to keep from killing them.

She caught her fingers on her lips again. Damn it. The man could kiss, but she'd not had the time to enjoy it more when he suddenly ripped—

Kylie stopped that train of thought. It was bad enough that she'd dreamed of the bastard all night, and now this. When her dad answered, she nearly cried.

"If you're calling again to tell me you're too sick to go, then I'm coming over there and beating your butt. I should have done it more when you were a kid, but now...well, I won't let you bail on your old man now." She sat down hard on her bed. "And you'd better be on time. No more 'just one more thing.' You know how you are, thinking you have all the time in the world, and you should've been dressed hours ago."

"I wasn't calling for that." He didn't believe her if the snort from the other end was any indication. "And I'm dressed. I have only to pull on my shoes, and I'm walking out the door." Which was another lie. She still had on the towel she'd had on for most of an hour. And the only thing she'd done to her long hair was brush out the tangles. It hung in a mass of curls down her back. Reaching behind her, she wondered if anyone would notice if she went bald.

"Dressed are you? Well, good. What is it you're wearing? I wish you'd have let me pay for your dress. No girl as pretty as mine should have to go in anything but the best."

She looked over at the dress she'd purchased in France with her first paycheck. Nearly all the first paycheck. She'd had such a good time there and hoped someday to be able to go back. But her daddy needed her, and she would move heaven and earth for him.

He'd done well for them. His father had left him a nearly broken newspaper, and her dad had brought it back to life. But he'd not changed when the world around him did. He'd waited nearly too long to realize that the computer age was here to stay. And now that subscriptions were way down, he was losing money and not able to upgrade to what they needed. She glanced over at the file that she and Daniel were to go over on Monday.

They wanted to take over her family's company and pay a hefty price to do so. The money was going to go a long way to getting the computers where they needed them to be. And all the employees, who'd not had a raise in nearly three years according to her dad, would be slightly compensated with the little extra money they'd have. Kylie hated it.

Not the proposal, but the man who'd come up with it was what terrified her really. She didn't think they needed his money, but her dad did. Well, not Curtis singly, but with the entire firm. And even though they had to sell some of their stock, they were selling it at a good market rate. She just didn't want to take it because of him.

Her fingers drifted to her mouth again. He'd kissed her. She couldn't get that out of her mind. When he'd stood before her and yanked her to his body, she'd been so shocked that, when his mouth had covered hers, she didn't know what to do. Her body did, though.

He'd devoured her mouth, ate at her until she'd surrendered to his tongue, and allowed it into her. Moaning, she'd been amazed he tasted so delicious and so hot. Before she could wrap her fingers through his hair and pull him closer, he pushed her away.

They were both breathing heavily. She could barely manage to catch her breath again when he spoke. Her hand was connecting with his cheek so quickly that she barely realized it was her. But a man did not tell a woman he was sorry after devastating her like he had.

Then without a word, he was gone. She couldn't move. Couldn't think beyond he'd kissed her, and she'd slapped him. When Daniel touched her shoulder, she'd done the most incredibly stupid thing and burst into tears. The one man she'd loved forever held her while she sobbed, and he suddenly wasn't what her body hummed for.

Her doorbell rang as she pulled her wrap off the hanger. She was late. And she hoped that whoever was at the door was here to help her zip her dress and not yell at her. She was sure it was going to be Curtis, and he was going to have a whip in his hand ready to… She wasn't sure what he'd be doing at her apartment, but she opened the door anyway. She almost choked on disappointment when it was Daniel.

If he noticed her look, he was polite enough not to say

anything. "You look lovely. But I'm thinking…do you need help?"

"Yes, please. I'm running behind again. And now my limo is going to cost me more, and then there is—" She slapped her hand over her mouth. She'd just blurted out part of their secret.

But again, Daniel was too polite to mention it. After she turned for him, he pulled the zipper up, only having it catch once. His fingers grazed her skin, and she shivered. It was nothing like when Curtis had—

She turned to him, smiling, then she frowned. "What are you doing here? I thought I told you I had a date with my dad." He reached for her wrap, and she allowed him to put it over her shoulders. "Daniel, what's going on?"

"Your dad called me. He said that he'd broken a button off his jacket, and the neighbor was sewing it on. Instead of making you both late, he asked if I could pick you up since my date bailed on me at the last minute. I told him that I would bring you, and he'd ride in later." He put out his arm for her to take. "Ready?"

The ride over was spent with the two of them talking. He never mentioned Curtis, and neither did she. Nor did he bring up the file. She was glad and hadn't realized until that second she'd needed this more than she'd thought. He smiled at her when the limo stopped but made no move to get out when the door opened.

"Curtis is going to be here tonight. Are you going to be all right with that?" She looked at the open door. "Kylie, what is the relationship between you two?"

That startled her. "We don't have…he kissed me, that's all. And then I slapped him. End of story. And even if things were different, you know as well as I do that I'm not his usual type."

Daniel nodded. Actually, Kylie had no idea what anyone's type was, but Daniel didn't seem to know that. She'd been gone until last month and now this.

"I'd like to see you. I know that we'll be working together on this project, but I'd very much like to take you out." Her heart flipped at his words. "You don't have to answer me now, but let me know."

She watched as he disappeared out of the limo and then reached back for her hand. She let him pull her out and then stood next to him as cameras went off all around them. She smiled, letting the moment take her. She finally had her dream man in her arms, and nothing would spoil it.

~~~

Curtis stood at the bar and watched them come in. He had already explained to his mother what he'd done and what he was going to do about it. She wasn't any happier about it than he was.

"You kissed her. Why?" He didn't answer, not that it mattered. "What does Daniel think? That girl has been in love with him for nearly all her young life."

"I know that. Da…darn it, Mom, why do you think…I'm not going to go tonight. I would embarrass her." He didn't add that he'd be hard pressed not to throw her over his shoulder and take her home with him. "I don't think we'll be able to come to an agreement if I make her too mad at me."

"You'll be there, young man, or you'll answer to me. And you're going to be nice to her. I don't care if it kills you." He thought it might. "And you'll not make Daniel mad either. He might want to settle down with this girl."

That statement was why he was hanging around at the bar listening to the mayor go on about pre-election planning and whatever else spewed from his mouth. When Daniel pulled the chair out for Kylie, Curtis excused himself and stepped outside at the back of the building. He nearly turned and went back when he saw Kylie's father, Jon Washington, standing there.

"Hello, Mr. Washington," Curtis said when the man caught him. "It's a little stuffy in there right now until everyone gets seated." He was babbling. He snapped his mouth closed and looked out across the lake that butted nearly up against the building. To the left of them was a beautiful eighteen hole golf course and to the right, the slightly smaller building that the city used for other functions. This building would hold more than a thousand, and it looked like it was nearly at capacity.

"It is. I don't care for these things anyway. Had to have your brother pick up Kylie so that I could get myself together a little more. Been years since I had to tux it up." He ran his hand down his jacket and fussed with a bit of lint. "My Betty used to love these things."

Curtis nodded. He remembered her, but not well. She'd died when Kylie had been about five or six. He turned to see Royce come out and nearly groaned. He had the look of a man who wanted answers.

"I've been looking for you." Royce directed his statement to both of them. "I was wondering if you've given any thought to what we've proposed."

"No, not really. I've been...I turned it all over to Kylie yesterday. She has all the information that you asked for. I understand that Daniel is going to be taking over from now on." Royce gave him a questioning look. "I hope you don't mind, but, well, I don't have the heart for it anymore. I've been a fool and now... well, now I just don't know what to do."

A few minutes later, Jon entered the party and, before Curtis could sneak in behind him, Royce stopped him. This was not going to go well he knew. His temper was getting the better of him, and he didn't want to be nice to anyone right now.

"Don't." Royce looked at him harder. "I mean it, Royce. I'm in no mood to explain things to you, and I certainly don't want to be around people right now."

"Mom said you'd kissed Kylie." That surprised Curtis though he wasn't sure why. They weren't a family that kept secrets well. "Feel like explaining that?"

"Nope." He moved toward the door again. "Daniel can handle the situation, and I'm going out of the country until next month. I want to be there to make sure the new building we put up in Europe finishes on time." He didn't have to be. They had the right people in the right jobs. And he knew that when he went, he'd more than likely be miserable as well as pissy. Which was fine by him. He was tired of being the nice guy.

The family table was crowded. There were several men standing and more sitting in the chairs around it. He saw his mom talking to the mayor as well as a few others from the state office there. Daniel nor Kylie was around, so he grabbed a chair when someone stood and ordered a drink.

"You still pouting?" He looked over at Kasey. "You've been in a nasty funk all day, and yesterday too. Is it because your brother got the job?" He didn't know what she was talking about and asked. "Royce managed to get that job in the governor's office. It's only a part-time thing, but he seems to be excited. I thought you were going to try for it."

"I decided that I didn't want the headache right now. I told Royce last week." He was glad now that he'd made that decision. "I'm going to Europe on Monday. I was wondering if I could have some little kiddy time before I left."

He watched little Lee, Royce, and Kasey's son, a couple hours a week. Kasey got some free time with her aunt Suzy, and he got to play with the little guy. He was nearly six months old now.

The meeting/dinner was called to order, and he was relieved to see that Daniel and Kylie weren't sitting with them. He was just getting relaxed when he noticed them coming toward them. Daniel was touching her back and guiding her to the table when he saw her stiffen. It was all he could do not go simply leave.

"Hello, everyone. I hope you don't mind, but Kylie's table has been overfilled. Mr. Taylor brought his wife and girlfriend. I think we might be safer over here. And I suppose being a tad late didn't help. Kylie had some zipper problems, and I had to help her with it." Daniel winked at him and sat her next to him as he sat on her other side. This was going to be a very long night.

"My goodness, Kylie, that dress is stunning. Where on earth did you get it?" Kasey kicked him under the table, and he winced. *What the hell was that for?* "Don't you think it's a lovely dress, Curtis?"

He looked at the dress in question. He did. And if the amount of drool he'd been wiping off his chin was any indicator, he'd be dehydrated for a month. He tried to think of something to say that didn't start with "I want to see it off you" and end with him in prison for killing the first man who looked at her. He looked at Kasey then back at Kylie. He was clueless, and he… "It's very pretty. It fits you nicely."

And it did too. The thing looked like it had been molded over her body and then tightened just a little bit more. Her hair was down a riot of curls that hung to her hips and made him want to ask her to turn so that he could see what she was hiding beneath it. But the front of the dress was what he was amazed by.

Black silk and pearls. The bodice held her so lovingly that he found himself jealous of the material. He could see her breasts as they overfilled the cups, and the lace that covered them did nothing but make him want to rip it from her. The long skirt flared slightly, and the long slit up her leg gave him a view of her long, luscious leg every time she took a step. He was kicked again when he realized he was staring.

"Thank you, Mr. Hunter." That hurt, though he was sure he deserved it. "I wasn't sure if it would be too light since it has gotten so cold."

Cold? Hardly. Especially sitting here with her. Curtis tried to think what the hell was wrong with him. He'd seen beautiful women before. Dated a lot of them because of events like this. He'd kissed a great number of them as well. But this woman, after one kiss, had gotten him so churned up that he wasn't sure what to do. He shifted in his chair again and looked at the now empty plate in front of him. Christ, had someone taken his food?

Everyone was still talking, and some were finished as well. He was glad. He hoped that he'd at least chewed with his mouth closed. Looking up, he watched Kylie place a bite of potato into her mouth. Her lips curled around the fork, and then her jaw moved in motion. He'd felt that mouth under his. And wanted to feel it move over his—

"I said, why don't you ask Kylie to dance?" He looked at Daniel and decided then and there the man was going to be killed tonight. "I have to go and meet with the mayor about that building they're selling off, and Kylie wants to dance."

He looked at her, and she shook her head. "No, that's not…I mean, I can wait until you get back. I don't want…need to dance with Curtis, Mr. Hunter. It'll be fine."

He stood up. "I'd love to dance with you." He walked around the table and pulled her chair back. "Come on, I promise not to step on your toes."

He was pissed that she'd not wanted to dance with him. He didn't particularly want to dance with her either, but that wasn't the point. The space where the band had been set up was across the room, and Curtis walked behind her just so he could see her ass sway. He was going to pay for this, and he just knew it.

Chapter 4

"What are you doing?" Daniel looked over at his mom. "You know that they had a fight yesterday, and I'm reasonably sure that they haven't resolved anything. Why would you force them together?"

He grinned and watched Curtis walk behind Kylie. The man had it bad. "I don't know what you're talking about, Mother dear. I simply asked my brother to dance with my date."

"That's another thing. Since when do you... Why you sly devil, you. You did this on...when did you figure it out?"

He looked at his mom again before answering. "When I was in Curtis' office yesterday. It wasn't until she slapped him that I realized that they were perfect for each other. You should have seen them together. Combustible." He took her hand into his and kissed the back of it. "If I make this work, will you leave me alone in your match-making ideas?"

"I most certainly do not know what you're going on about." She flushed, and he knew he had her. "Besides, they're only dancing. I wouldn't be crowing just yet."

Daniel spent nearly two hours on his plan. First, was to

get them together alone. Well, that had been a bust tonight, but the night was still young. And he'd make his brother jealous. In this case, more jealous. He'd seen the way Curtis had watched her every move. And Kylie wasn't much better. He'd nearly fallen off his chair when she called him Mr. Hunter.

"If he finds out what you're up to, he's not going to be happy." His mom was right, but he hoped by then it would be too late. "And if this works, I'm going to give you a reprieve, but you're not off the hook."

He could live with that. He figured the rate his brother and Kasey were going, they'd have another kid before the end of the next year. And if he managed to get Curtis and Kylie together, they'd reproduce within the next couple as well. He looked around the table at his other brother.

No hope for Jesse. The man dated more than he did, and he had a rule that he never broke. No marriage. Ever. But that didn't mean he couldn't be tempted. So long as everyone left him alone, he was willing to take a few punches for the cause. He glanced over at Kasey and Royce. No one could find a love like theirs.

They'd had a bumpy start. And when Kasey's mom had passed away, everyone thought that it would be over for the two of them. Then Kasey had ended up pregnant. And now they were supposed to work with Kasey to get a good-will ad put into the papers as well as saving the company. Daniel knew just how he was going to work that meeting, as well.

Yeppers, life was going to be a long road for a while, but he was going to enjoy it. He leaned back in his chair and winked at the woman at the other table. Yep, things were going to be very fun.

~~~

The dance had to be the longest one in history. She was stiff in his arms and wouldn't speak to him beyond a few grunts, and a couple of I don't knows. He'd had enough.

"When did you get home?" Nothing. "Are you going back to wherever you came from soon after the deal is closed?" She hesitated a second, and he knew she was going to speak, but all he got was a glare and his toes mashed.

Looking around at the other couples, all five of them, he thought about what he wanted to do to the one he was sort of holding. Spanking her came to mind. Then that thought brought up all sorts of images. None of which were helping. Maybe if he simply found a nice corner, took her there, and kissed her until he had her out of his system. He was pretty sure that kissing wouldn't be enough, but he wanted to try. Looking around the room again, he thought he found the perfect place. Stopping, he looked down at her.

"Come with me. We're going to have this out right now." Wrapping his arm around her waist and practically dragging her to the small door he knew lead to a small office, he was thrilled to find it unlocked. Opening the door, he shoved her inside and then shut the door behind them.

"What do you think you're doing? You let me out of here this minute. I'm here with your brother." He moved toward her, and she took several steps back to avoid him.

"No. And are you dating him now?" She looked confused for a moment, and he had his answer. "I can see that you want to, but you and I have unfinished business."

"What business could we possibly have?" She bumped against the desk and had to stop. He didn't. "You need to stop moving right...what is it you think we have to talk about?"

He took off his jacket and tossed it on the chair. "I didn't say we were going to talk. I said we have unfinished business.

I think if I were to get you out of my system, maybe taste you, then I'll be able to move on."

That didn't even sound nice to his ears. And when she drew back her hand to hit him, he grabbed it, pulled it behind her, and then her body was flush with his. Her breathing changed immediately, as did his. She was where he needed her to be, and he wanted to begin his purging now.

Leaning slowly to her mouth, he moaned when she licked her full lower lip. He took the damp morsel into his own lips and nibbled. Her hand moved from the desk behind her to his forearms.

"When I kissed you yesterday, I was angry. I'm not sure why, but…" He ran his tongue over the seam of her mouth and then flicked it into her. "But I was. Kissing you seemed a better idea than to spank you."

Letting go of her hand behind her, Curtis ran his hand down her bared back to the curve of her ass. Sliding further, he cupped her and brought her closer to him. Her answering moan had him pressing her into the desk as he lifted her up.

"Please, Curtis. Please. I need you to…you have to not want this." He knew she was right, but it was much too late for that now.

"Let me in, Kylie. Let me taste you again. Let me feel your mouth under mine and your tongue touching me." Curtis lifted her higher and heard a tearing sound. Her dress, her dress wasn't up to the way he wanted her. And he wanted her now.

Setting her on the desk, her ass as near the edge as he could make it without her sitting in the middle, he dropped to his knees in front of her. He was going to have his fill of her if it was the last thing he did. Running his hands from her ankles to her knees, he watched her face.

When the dress was just below her hips, he stopped. Her whimpering had him nearly smile, but he didn't want her to think he was winning. Right now, he didn't feel like a winner so much as the king of the world. Then he found the top of her thigh-high stockings.

"Do you have any idea how sexy these are to me?" He almost didn't recognize his voice and kissed the top of her thigh, were the band on her stocking stopped. "I love a woman in these. It makes your legs look incredibly sexy as well as not hiding what treasures you have just above them."

"Curtis. Please stop talking and take me. I'm so wet right now. I'm sure that you can see it." His cock twitched at her pleading. "Please, just do it."

"So impatient. What if I told you that I can not only see how wet you are but smell you too?" He lifted the dress to her waist and saw the garter as well as the smallest panties he'd ever seen. They barely covered her mound. He leaned in and kissed the skin just above her panties.

He was going to have to do something soon or come in his pants. While coming inside of her was what he really wanted, he knew that he couldn't go that far. Watching her face, he wound his fingers into her panties and tore them from her.

Her climax startled him. She didn't come hard, nor did she make much in the way of noise. But he was going to change that. He wanted her to scream out when she came, and he was going to drink all he could from her when she did. As soon as he put this mouth to her skin again, she gripped the back of his head.

Nothing could have prepared him for her taste. She was warm and wet, tasty, and sweet. He wanted to make her come again and again. Worrying her clit, he adjusted himself until he was able to reach his cock. Freeing it from his trousers was paradise, but short lived. He needed to give himself as much relief as he hoped she'd get. Grabbing his cock and stroking it, he devoured her pussy until she came again. Then a third time.

When she begged him to stop, he couldn't help but give her one more. And he realized then that it was never going to be enough. Leaning back from her, he fisted his cock and watched her tremble.

"Are you going to come like that?" Her voice was thick and hoarse. He watched her as she sat on the desk and leaned back. "Stand up, Curtis. It's my turn."

He shook his head. "No. I won't be able to stop if you put your mouth on me. And if you were to touch me right now, I'd want to come down your throat." Curtis felt his balls tighten and wanted more than anything to come inside of her still dripping pussy. When she stood up and turned around on the desk, he leaned in and nipped at her ass. When she moaned again and moved back to him, he knew that coming with his hand wasn't going to do. The pretty ass in front of him was about to get all of him.

"Have you ever had anyone in your ass, Kylie?" Her no had him whimper. "I want to fuck you there hard while I spank you. Would you like that, baby?"

"Yes, please. I need you. I need your cock." She moved back against his cock, and he watched as a long stream of his pre-cum dripped onto her. Taking his cock into his hand, he reached around her and gathered her cream onto his fingers. Bringing it to her ass, he slid it up and down her crack.

"I can't take you now, baby. I don't have any protection. But I can come on you. Please tell me it's all right. Let me come all over your beautiful ass." She nodded and moaned again.

Sliding his cock into her ass, he squeezed her cheeks onto his cock. The friction wasn't as good as he knew her pussy would be, but it felt fantastic. When she reached between her own thighs and started to ride her fingers, Curtis knew he was done for. His cock jerked in her ass once, then again, until he erupted all over her. Her answering climax had him reach down to her fingers and slide them into her, deep into her pussy until she came again around both their fingers. Curtis could barely move when she finally drew a deep breath. Then he thought about what they'd just done.

What the hell was he doing? He had just fucked his brother's date. And not only that, but he'd fucked her in a dirty office that had cigarette butts in an ashtray. He moved back off her and looked around for something to clean them up with. Kylie moved to the side of the desk, holding up her dress, and tore three tissues out of the box sitting there. He took them from her and asked her to turn.

"We shouldn't have done this. I'm so sorry, but I shouldn't have done this. You're my brother's girlfriend." It was easier for him to say what he was because she couldn't see him. "This is all my fault, and I shouldn't have let…I have…I'm sorry, Miss Washington."

He'd meant it as a way to put distance between them. He did that all right and pissed her off too. She turned so quickly that he thought she was going to hit him, and this time he would have welcomed it.

"Get out." Her voice was like poison, icy poison, and he was going to be dead from it. "I want you to do whatever you need to do, then get away from me. If you so much as say my name, even if I'm not around, I will hunt you down and cut that useless appendage off and feed it to you."

"Now wait a fucking minute. You enjoyed that as much

as I did. You could have said no." He hoped that he would have been able to stop or to turn her to his way of thinking. But right now, this moment, he wasn't so sure.

She picked up the box of tissues and tossed them at him. He was glad he'd been able to catch it. He would have hated to have to explain what he'd been doing to get a goose egg on his forehead.

"Kylie, listen to me. I only meant that—" When she picked up the stapler and held it like she was going to throw it, he backed off. Her dress was back in place before he straightened up. He figured that she'd forgotten her panties, and, when she stormed to the door, he picked them up and put them into his pocket. He was only behind her by less than three minutes, but she must have been running because when he came out behind her, he couldn't find her.

He didn't want to have to go back to the table and try to explain how he'd lost her. But after searching in vain for nearly ten minutes, he finally went back to his table. She and Daniel were just leaving.

"I'm taking Kylie home. She has a migraine and wants to go to bed to sleep it off. I'll probably stay with her tonight to make sure she's all right."

He wanted to tell his brother he was getting sloppy seconds, but didn't. He wanted to also confess to his brother what he'd forced her to do. Because he knew that's just what he'd done. She'd never actually said the words to him, but he felt as if he forced her all the same. He was such a prick.

As much as he wanted to leave, he made himself stay to the end. The thought of going home to his empty house, or even his empty office, to work was depressing. He watched the speeches without hearing them and tried too hard to pretend to be normal. Which he was pretty sure he never was going to be again.

When he fell into bed at a little after five in the morning, he hoped he'd fall to sleep. And he did for the first three or so hours. Then, after that, he tossed and turned so much that he got up and went to watch some television. Nothing on but an agricultural station and movies he'd seen so much he could recite the dialogue by heart.

He spent most of Sunday trying to pay attention to the game on the idiot box. Television just wasn't what it used to be. Then he'd done a couple of loads of laundry, avoiding the phone every time it rang. He didn't feel like socializing and knew that if he ended up at his mom's like she'd been asking him to do all morning, Kylie would be there. By nine that night, he went to bed.

Chapter 5

Kylie watched Daniel struggle through the file. She just wanted to get this over with and go home. There was a gallon of ice cream she'd not finished off the day before, and she wanted to dig into it. She looked up at Daniel when he sighed.

"I have to call Curtis again. I'm sorry. I won't be a minute." He picked up the phone, and she looked away. She wouldn't react to knowing that he was nearby. It was bad enough she'd parked outside the building for thirty minutes, hoping to see him. She shuddered.

The call didn't last long, and Kylie thought maybe there had been a small tiff between the men. She'd heard the loud voice on the other end and had had to work hard on not leaping over the desk and grabbing the phone.

This went on for nearly an hour. Daniel would read a little and call his brother. She was beginning to think that Daniel wasn't the lawyer she'd thought him to be when suddenly the door slammed open, and Curtis came in.

Kylie looked at Daniel. She could swear that she heard him say, "It's about fucking time," but not with complete certainty. She stood up to go when Curtis barked at Daniel.

"It's all right there. Fucking read it. I swear to Christ, if you call me once more about this thing, I'm going to brain you." He took some papers from the desk and then slammed them back in front of Daniel. "See, right there. I told you twice. I even told you what page, paragraph, and line."

"Then do it yourself." Daniel stood up, grabbed his jacket, and left the room, slamming the door behind him. Both she and Curtis stared at each other, neither of them moving.

She picked up her purse and coat and moved to the door. She didn't want to do this at all, and she certainly wasn't going to do it with him. She stopped when Curtis spoke.

"Your father is broke. Not just broke, but he can't meet payroll this week. He barely did last week." She turned to him. "If you don't sign this deal, you both will lose everything."

"You lie. My father has been running this business since he got it from his father. He could buy and sell you twice over." She had no idea how much the Hunters were worth, but she'd bet it was more than they had at the moment.

"I don't lie. Ask him. And at one time, your father was a great businessman, but he let things slip, things that should have been upgraded. The computers, for one thing, the building for another."

"And what do you think you can do to help him? Come in with guns blazing and make it all right for him? I doubt that. You're a selfish prick." She tried to pull in her temper, but it was too late. "I'd rather live on the streets than to—"

"You've said that before, and you will too. As well as your father. He mortgaged everything, including the house you live in and his. The cars will be taken today if..." He picked up the papers off his brother's desk. "Take them to him, Kylie. Ask him. Tell him what I said and have him deny it."

"If what?" He turned away and gathered the papers. She

wanted to jerk them from him and burn them. "If what? What will you do to keep the creditors at bay?"

"I can pay them off." She stared at him, not understanding what he was saying. But he explained. "I own the place where he bought them. I know...I've known for some time that your family has been having money problems."

"You bought the dealership to own my dad?" As soon as the words left her mouth, she knew they weren't true. "I'm sorry. That was uncalled for."

He handed her the file he'd had and took several steps back. She looked at him, and her body seemed to want him to make a move to her. But her mind kept thinking about him telling her he was sorry. She turned toward the door and left without another word. She rode the elevator down, trying not to think, not to feel. She was in her car when she called her dad.

"Hello, darling. How was your meeting with Daniel?" He chuckled. "Did you get all the business things worked out?"

She leaned her head back against the headrest and closed her eyes. "It was mostly with Curtis. Dad...how bad is it?"

He didn't answer right away, and she brushed at the tears on her cheeks. He cleared his throat several times before he began.

"Bad. More than bad, it's...we're going to lose it all. I know that if I sell to the Hunters, they'll...I guess I hoped that they'd bail me out enough where the staff would at least get their last checks. I'm sorry, baby. I didn't want to tell you."

"How long? How long have you known?" She knew that she wasn't going to like the answer, but she needed to know how long the Hunters had known. "When did you realize that if you didn't sell, it would be gone?"

"Seven years."

Seven years. Since she'd gone to grad school. Since she'd spent time in Paris. Since... "Dad, why didn't you tell me? I would have helped, I would have...I would have done things differently."

She heard him sniffle and knew that her strong, vibrant dad was crying. She wanted to go to him, wanted to pull him into her arms and tell him it would be all right. She looked up at the big building she was next to and knew that there lay the only answer.

"I wanted you to be young. Carefree. I wanted to give you everything. I didn't...I knew what I was doing. But I thought I could fix it. Make it right. But I couldn't. Then it got to be...I failed you."

"No, Dad. We failed each other." She looked at the building again. "I'll be home later. I have to go...I have something I need to do."

He told her he loved her and hung up. She looked in the mirror on her visor and fixed her makeup. When you were going to grovel, it was best, she thought, to look good. Getting out of the car, she took the file with her. Even stopping at the security desk took too little time. She was led to the elevator by the same Officer York.

"It can't be all that bad, miss. The Hunters are a good bunch. Noisy and a little headstrong, but they have good hearts." She nodded, and when the door opened, he spoke again. "You'll be fine. Just let them help you."

When she got to the desk outside of Curtis' office, he was waiting. She knew that the guard had called him. He let her go into his office in front of her, and she sat down. She pulled out the file from her purse.

"Where do I sign? I have Dad's power of attorney, and I'm ready to sign it over to you." He didn't move. She was afraid that he'd changed his mind. "I want to do this. I have to do this."

The door behind them opened, and Royce and Mrs. Hunter walked in. She turned to look at Curtis, embarrassed beyond words.

"I have another plan. They have to be...we all own this company, but Mom and Royce are the major holders. They have to approve it before we can move on." Mrs. Hunter sat next to her, and Royce stood against the wall behind his brother's desk.

"I don't want another plan. I want to finish this so that I can...I guess I'll have to move out. My dad and I will. We'll have to find an apartment somewhere. Cheap, I guess." She closed her mouth to stop the flow of words that they could care less about. "I'm sorry. I'm a little overwhelmed right now."

Suddenly, she was sick. Not just sick, but ready to throw up. She put her hand over her mouth, and Curtis stood and showed her where the bathroom was. She barely made it and didn't really have time to lock the door before she was kneeling before the commode and throwing up hard.

~~~

"Poor girl. She didn't know, did she?" Curtis knew that his mom didn't require an answer, and he didn't have one. He'd been telling Jon to tell his daughter for weeks. "I like your plan. Do you think she'll accept?"

"She doesn't have much of a choice." He looked at Royce. He sounded as sorry as Curtis felt. "You'll have to convince her to do this."

Curtis wondered when it had become his job. But he wanted to help her. He looked toward the bathroom and wondered if she needed anything. His mom picked up the telephone and ordered some tea and crackers from the dining room.

Royce paced. He had come in case Curtis needed to convince her. When Jay had called to tell him she wanted to come up, he was nervous. He thought for sure she was going to say that she'd rather live in her car again or some other nonsense. Like he'd let that happen. When the door opened from the bathroom, he looked at her.

She was pale, and her eyes were red. When she staggered slightly, Royce got to her first. She tried to brush him off.

"I'm fine. Just…I don't think I remembered to eat breakfast again." He picked up the phone and ordered her the special. "I'm not hungry. Please, can't we just get this over with? I need to get home and…I need to get home."

Curtis nodded. But he did ask to have the food sent up for both him and her as soon as possible. He'd missed lunch too. When she sat down, both he and his brother did.

"We're not going to close you down. Not entirely anyway. We're going to set up your company up in one of our buildings. All new computers, as well as someone there to train you how to use them, how to set up the company so that you can go online right away." He waited for her to say something and he nearly smiled when she did. He didn't want her to hurt him.

"You're not going to shut us down and give us computers." She snorted. "Why would you do that?"

"Because we'll own the company, at least most of it, and we'll make it make a profit." Royce handed her another sheet of paper. "This is what you're in debt for. We'll pay all this off, as well as take the building. It's not worth as much as it says on paper, but we can use it. Once we get it back up to code, if your business is doing better, we'll move you back into it if you want."

"My business. You just said that you'd be the owners. I won't own jack." She looked at their mom. "You agree with this? Even though you're going to take on a great deal more debt than the paper is worth, you still want to do this?"

Mom looked at him and Royce. The knock at the door gave them a little time to answer. He didn't have a clue how to tell her what they'd already done, and, when he did, she was going to be more pissed than ever. His mom bullied her into sitting at the small conference table while he sat at his desk. And where the hell was Daniel?

He'd called him or had tried to call him as soon as Kylie had come back. He picked up his cell phone to see if he'd called. Nothing. As he ate his sandwich, he thought about Kylie and how best to tell her the list of things he'd already put into motion. He thought the best way was to simply tell her.

"We've already paid off your father's house. Yours, we couldn't because it's in the business name and not on a personal loan. The car is also paid, and the salary for the next three months is covered." She stared at him and didn't speak. He moved down his list. "The taxes are paid up to date and—"

"Taxes? You mean he hadn't been…how long have the taxes been behind? Close to seven years by any chance?" He looked up at her from his notes and nodded. "That's what I thought."

"Kylie, it's not as bad as you think. We'll close down for a little while and reopen with—"

She cut Royce off. "You said that I only had to sign off on this, correct? Sign the papers, and you'd have it all?" Curtis didn't move except to look at Royce. "Answer me, damn it."

"That's the way the contract is worded, yes, but I've made

some changes on it, so it'll reflect what you owe as well. We'll make sure that your house is paid off and that—"

"I don't want it. I don't want anything for me. I appreciate you seeing to my dad, but as for me…" She stood up. "Where do I sign, Mr. Hunter? I want to sign it and leave. I have a great deal to do and very little time…could we please simply get this over with?"

Curtis looked at his family, and they stood as well. When the door closed behind them, he moved to the front of his desk and asked her to have a seat. She paused for so long that he thought she'd leave and not let him talk, but she finally sat down. He wanted more than anything to pull her into his arms and hold her. She'd been through a great deal in the past few days, and he felt horrible for being the biggest part of her misery.

"We want to help you. We have the resources as well as the capital. We are always looking for ways to expand, and this is simply one more thing to move in that direction." He saw the tears in her eyes and decided that the pat answer that they gave every buy-out wasn't what he wanted to say to her. "Did you know that your dad gave me my first job? He let me deliver papers and paid me too much to do it. I had a great sense of ethics as well as a strict mom. She said there is no job that you shouldn't give your all."

"Dad said that he knew your father. He said there was never a man in this world that loved his family like he did." She reached for a tissue on his desk. "What does this have to do with me signing the papers? You've no idea how much I just want to go home, crawl into a deep corner, and wait for this nightmare to be over."

"It doesn't have to be a nightmare." She laughed a bitter, short bark. "It doesn't. Kylie, we're going to need someone to run the paper. We're going to have to have someone take the people from one kind of reporting to the next level. We know that you can do it."

"I don't want it." This time when she stood, he did as well. "Either I sign the papers, or I sell to the man who's been calling my dad to sell to him for months. I don't care anymore. Please, give me this."

He nodded and decided he'd talk to her dad. He'd be able to convince her to do what they'd set up for her. After she signed, she left. Not another word, not even a goodbye. He cursed his brother Daniel for not being here for her when she needed it.

Curtis put the contract in the file and took it to his brother. Royce, like all of them, had law degrees and something more. Curtis' second career was that of a cook. Le Cordon Bleu, as a matter of fact. Royce's was real estate. He put the file on his desk and headed for the door, but his brother stopped him before he could touch the door.

"She doesn't know, does she?" He turned to look at him. "She has no idea that *you,* not the company, just bought her father's newspaper and his house, does she?"

He shrugged. "What does it matter? It's done. And if it makes as much profit as I think it will, I might sell it to you."

"You keep it. Have you told her that you love her?" Curtis looked at Royce, shocked. "You've been in love with her since we were kids, and she was the biggest pain in the ass known to man…or at least four teenage boys who couldn't shake her. Are you going to tell her?"

"She's in love with Daniel." He turned to the door again. "Take the red flag off the plane, Royce. I let it go today because I wanted to make sure that this went the way I wanted it to go, but now it's done. Don't ground the plane again, or I'll simply buy a ticket and fly commercial."

"I thought you knew it was us. You gave in too easily when I told you this morning." He heard Royce's chair creak. "Please don't go, Curtis. The project overseas can wait until it's closer to completion."

"I have to. For the reasons you named and those you don't know." He turned back to look at him. "Yes, you're right. I'm in love with her. But I know that I don't stand a snowball's chance in hell with her in love with Daniel. And I won't step on something that could be just for him." He walked out of the office and bypassed his own. He walked out of the front and up the street. He was nearly four blocks from the offices when his cell phone went off. He simply ignored it and turned and headed back to the office. After checking in with his secretary, he told her to hold his calls.

Chapter 6

"Yes, Daddy, I know, but this is the best way. It'll be nice for you to be here and not have to run the paper anymore." She heard the words, but her heart was closed to them. "You'll enjoy having a great deal of time to do the things you wanted." She'd gone straight to his house and didn't tell him what had happened. All she'd told him was that he'd no longer have to worry about the paper or the bills that plagued him. Nor would he have to worry about her. She was going to California and staying there. She thought she could find a job easily enough.

"I don't know why you thought it was a burden all these years. I met your mom there and that, as far as I'm concerned, is the greatest thing about it." He pulled her to his couch and looked at her. She could never hide anything from him. "What happened? You know that you want to, just tell me what happened."

She tried to look away, but he wouldn't have it. "Dad, you should have told me that the paper was in such bad shape. I didn't know anything all these years."

"I didn't want you to stop having fun and come here to

help me. Your mother and I wanted you to enjoy life before you had to be forced to get a job and work for the rest of it. You had a good time and now…well, now it's time for someone else to take the helm. And I think the Hunter Corporation will do a fine job. I even put in that they hire you, or there was no deal."

She wondered if that was why they had offered her the job, but dismissed it almost immediately. They were too good at what they did, and hiring someone they knew wasn't something they'd do.

She got up to pace, but the phone ringing startled her. Her dad was probably the only person in the world that still had a house phone. She only knew of businesses that did any more. Picking up the receiver, she also noted that it was a dial kind, not even press buttons for her dad.

"Hello." The silence at the other end had her nearly hang up, but the voice made the hair on her arms stand.

"Miss Washington. So nice to speak to you. It's Eric Howe. I was wondering if I could have a word with your father? It's about the paper. I want to up my offer to him." She looked over at her dad as the man continued. "Tell him that I'm willing to pay ten percent over my last offer."

"I'm sorry, Mr…what did you say your name was?" She wrote a note to her dad that simply said, *Eric?* "Never mind. Dad and I have decided to go with someone else."

"That's not very nice of you. I've been asking for months to buy it. I would like to know who you think you're selling it to so that I can make them a better offer." He laughed. "It will be at a greater loss for me, but I'm willing to take the hit."

"I'm sorry, but it's a done deal. Thank you for calling. Have a nice day." She hung up the phone and looked at her dad. "Who is this person? And why does he think we should give him the Hunters' name so he can buy the paper?"

"I've no idea. He's been a pain in my bottom for a while now. Usually, I just don't answer until he calls so much I get a head pain." Her dad went to the cabinet to get down mugs for some tea he was brewing. "Come on. Sit down and tell me what you and the Hunters have decided."

"They've fixed it so that payroll is going to be met. And this house is paid off from the mortgage as well as the back taxes. And…Dad, why didn't you tell me? I know what you said, but it's bigger than me having a carefree life. This is more like you've simply let it go."

He sat down and blew over his mug. He'd been using this mug since she'd given it to him when she'd been ten. It was nicked and cracked at the rim and handle, but he used it all the time.

"I guess I sort of did. I'd been talking with Curtis for years now. He's a good boy. Did you know that he's just like his own father? Royce looks like their dad, but Curtis is just like him in both mannerism as well as temperament. Shy too. But when he saw me…well, he knew right away that things weren't going well. He even tried to get me to make some improvements back awhile ago." He got up and pulled down the cookie tin he told her that her mother used when she baked. "Those are from Mrs. Dillard from across the street. She's sort of sweet on me. Anyway, where was I?"

She knew who Mrs. Dillard was. Kylie was a little shocked that the woman was "sweet" on her dad. She had thought the woman old when she'd been a child, but now she must be in her hundreds if she was a day. Then she looked at her dad. He'd aged too. She realized that he should be aged; he was nearly eighty. He'd been twenty years older than her mom when they'd married, and they'd had her very late in his life.

She reached out and took his hand into hers.

"I love you, Daddy." He blushed brightly and kissed her hand holding his. "You were telling me about Mr. Hunter."

"No, I wasn't. I was talking about young Curtis. But I'll let it go for now." She didn't know what he meant, but he moved on. "The computers were the least of my problems. There were taxes and costs. When the price of gas went up so high, everything went up with it. Paper costs nearly tripled. Then there were the costs of delivering papers to the people who wanted them mailed to them. We have a lot of subscribers who live out of state. It was difficult to keep it up. Then Milton passed."

It took her several moments to remember who Milton was. He'd been her dad's secretary. She'd been told he'd passed away about ten years ago. Had even come home for the funeral, but she didn't know what he'd had to do with the paper going to pot.

"He knew everything about the computers. He could find me deals on whatever I needed. And I didn't realize how much...when he died, it seemed as if he was my last friend that knew your mother as I had. After his passing...well, I simply didn't care. I tried, but I just didn't have it in me anymore."

He looked away from her, but not before she saw the tears. Before she could speak, the phone rang, and she got up to answer it. It was that man again.

"I can go to fifteen percent over my last offer, but not a penny more. How do I know that you have another offer? You might be trying to get more money off me, and I'm simply not going to be had."

"I already told you that I have an offer. In fact, we've already signed off on the deal. Stop calling here and bothering my dad." She hung up before he could speak. And when the phone rang again almost immediately, her dad told her to ignore it. She tried, but finally, they moved to the living room where she gathered her things. "I have to go home. I have some things I have to do. Don't talk to that man again. He's annoying."

"I won't. You drive carefully on the way home. I love you, sweetheart." She hugged him and told him she loved him too.

Now that she was alone in her car, she thought back to the meeting this morning. She'd been a poor businesswoman there in front of them. She pulled out her cell intending to order a pizza for dinner to pick up when she saw she had four missed calls. She didn't know the number and wondered who it had been. Listening to the voicemail, she realized that it was Daniel, and he'd invited her out for dinner. She debated for all of a minute and called him back to tell him no. She was tired and needed to start packing. She didn't know how much longer she had before the bank took her home.

"I won't take no for an answer," he said when he answered. "You simply let me come and get you, and we'll talk about nothing but how beautiful you've become and how handsome I am. Then if you're a really good girl, I'll take you to Samuel's Ice Cream Bar to get a decadent dessert."

She laughed and realized that she really didn't want to go home to pack. She told him that she was near the pizza place on Main Street and asked if he could meet her there.

"Of course. I'm around the corner now. I was thinking someplace more dark and romantic, but pizza does sound good." She pulled into the parking place as he continued. "Maybe later, we can go back to my place and go over whatever questions you might have about the buyout."

She looked at the lot she was sitting in and wondered

why the thought of him wanting to take her back to his place didn't appeal to her as much as it once had. "I have some things to do tonight and...well, I think your brother answered everything all right."

He had too. He'd been more than helpful. And the deed to her dad's house was one of them. It had been delivered while she'd been there. Her father had cried and told her it was more than he'd expected. She'd had to lie to him about her getting a similar envelope, telling him she'd already had what he'd offered her. Which she supposed was truer than not.

Daniel pulled in beside her before she could think of much more. Getting out of her car, she had a fleeting thought as to if it would be there when she returned. Her dad had told her that the creditors had been asking for the vehicle or the money for three months now. She opened the door and took out her laptop bag, as well as her jacket, and held them to her with her purse. These things, she couldn't replace.

Daniel took the bag and held the door open for her when they entered the noisy place. This isn't what she'd wanted all those years ago, but it might be what she needed now. They both ordered a beer after being shown to their table and settling in.

"So," Daniel started. "Tell me if you still love me, or do you love my brother? Frankly, he's a much better catch."

~~~

Eric glared at the phone. He wanted to call again. But he knew from experience when dealing with the old man, and now apparently the daughter, that calling back would get him nowhere. Once they said something was finished, it was as good as dead. Like the man in the corner.

Eric Howe was a man who demanded perfection, loyalty,

and respect. He never gave those things in return, but he did demand them of those he considered less than him. Which, to his way of thinking, was everyone else in the world. The man in the corner was one of those he'd made demands of, and he hadn't followed through. It wasn't any more Eric's fault than it had been the gun that had killed him. The man simply had not performed the way Eric had expected him to.

And now the Washingtons were failing him too. And the little girl thinking that she could make offers on his building without him saying so was not going to fly with him. He looked at the picture on his desk. This, too, was the fault of his past family members.

Had they simply paid the taxes on the building or, better yet, not gotten caught and sent to prison, the building and what it held would be his. His grandfather had owned the big building on Biloxi Avenue and had lost it to the taxman long ago. And now it was within his grasp once again, but a woman was in the way.

Eric didn't care what problems the paper had. He could care less about the people that worked there and less about the people who owned it. Or thought they did. As far as he was concerned, it was simply a piece of paper that kept him from the money that he knew was in one of the walls. Money that his stupid father had hidden there when the bank robbery they'd been in on had gone bad.

The man had told him nearly three years ago as he lay dying on his floor about it all. He said that Eric could have the money if he'd just let him live. Eric had promised him he'd take care of him as soon as he told him.

"We were being chased, your grandda and I. The police were hot on our tails, and we had to get rid of the money or face a bigger jail sentence than we might have. He should never have killed that cop. Cops don't like it when you take out one of their own." Eric knew this to be true. This was why he was calling himself Eric Howe instead of his real name of Vaughn LaMancusa. "It's all there. We left it there all these years as a sort of nest egg if you want to call it. All of it. We didn't even have time to split it with the others. Not that it mattered, the cops had already taken care of that problem for us."

"How much?" When he didn't answer quickly enough for him, he hit him again. "How much is there? And why wasn't I ever told about it?"

The cold laughter made his skin crawl. He and his father had never gotten along, and that morning was simply the breaking point. He hit his father again and watched the blood pour from his mouth. He was as good as dead, and they both knew it.

All he'd wanted was to have his own territory to run. He'd felt that being the number two man on the payroll had been going on long enough. Especially in light of the fact that Eric had killed off the number one guy that morning. He wanted to be able to expand into things his father hadn't wanted. Drugs, for one, and also prostitution, as well as a few other things his father had always stayed away from. And when he'd laughed at him, well, Eric had never been known for a cool head.

"You'd have blown it up your nose, and, if that didn't work, then you would have gotten us caught." The laughter again pissed him off. "Besides, you've never been worth a fucking thin dime since you spewed from your mother's pussy."

He thought about it later and knew that his father had made him kill him. He'd been in a great deal of pain, Eric knew. He'd done the damage to him all by himself. But killing his father hadn't gotten him shit, and now that the building was this close, the fucking bastard was still laughing at him. He should have taken a deep breath and let him suffer more, but he'd broken his neck then and, in the way of their family, had sawed his head off along with his hands. When he had some problems with the tongue, he'd simply left the pieces of it on the corpse and walked away after tossing the house. Throwing the head and hands in the dumpster had been another bad move, but it was done now, and Eric had moved on.

The money in his father's desk drawer, as well as the money and jewels he'd found throughout the house, had been a nice payday. About ten million in cash and gold. There might have been more, but he didn't know the combination to the safe and was pretty sure his father had planned it that way. Whenever he'd asked him for it, he'd tell him that the lawyer was the only one who knew it and he'd been out of town.

Eric had found the lawyer afterward, and the man hadn't known dick. And Eric had given him every opportunity to tell him too. Right up until he'd severed his head as well. Over the years, nearly ten now, he'd gotten much better at what he liked to call his signature. Having to kill off so many idiots in his father's employment had helped on that score. But now he was nearly broke.

It had taken him nearly a decade to figure out what his father had been talking about. The bank robbery had happened nearly about the time he'd been born thirty years ago. His father had been a bank/anything else robber since before he'd met his mom. Then, as the years had gone by, with the money not going as far, he'd taken to going into bigger banks and taking more cash until he'd been nearly caught. Then the man had simply been a doormat and had been doing small shit since shortly before his death.

Now what? He had to get the building. According to the article, and it had been a piss poor one at that, there were three people dead, two of them cops and one a bank manager, and an undisclosed amount of money. Undisclosed? What kind of bank didn't know how much money was in it? He wanted to scream at the paper for such shitty work, but he couldn't afford to piss off the family any more until he had the building, then the money first.

Who would she have sold it to? No one around here had enough money for it. And there was the added knowledge that the place was falling down around their ears. Someone stupid enough to pay more than he'd offered must have known about the money too.

He sat down at his desk and looked at the phone. Someone had to know. He pulled the phone toward him and then searched for a phonebook. He was still looking when his cook came in with his lunch tray. He asked her if she knew how to find out who had purchased a building that had been for sale.

"They put those in the paper on Sunday. All the transfers, I mean. It sometimes takes a bit if there's only one or two. But it gets in there mostly on time. Who you looking for?"

Mary Phyllis had been working for him long enough not to ask questions about most things. Like the body in the corner. Eric knew that she'd seen it. Her pause with the tray at the door told him that, but she'd not said a word and had acted like it was nothing out of the ordinary.

"The newspaper on Biloxi Avenue. I've heard that it was bought recently and was wondering who might have bought it."

She looked at him strangely, then finished her task.

"Didn't know it was for sale. I knew the owners were having some problems. Hard to live in this town without hearing everything." She held out his chair for him as he moved to the little table he always used. "I'll keep my ear out. Might be some bigger company that wants to keep it close to the vest. But I'll get it for you."

She moved out of the room, pausing again at the doorway to look over at the body. She told him that she'd have that mess taken care of pronto and went out, closing the door behind her. Eric threw back his head and laughed. She'd made it sound as if there was a spot on the carpet and that she'd have it cleaned right away. He decided that she needed a raise and tucked into his lunch.

Tomorrow he'd see what he could find out about the Washington girl and her old man. Then he'd start to see about making some…changes at the Washington building, beginning with setting some small fires and hoping for a large scale one. Nothing like a burnt out shell of a building to get someone to back off of what he'd come to think of as his.

Eric ignored the man who came in and picked up the body. He also ignored Mary when she came in to fuss over the real stains on the floor. But the smell of cleaning fluids he could not ignore. He gathered up his coat and phone and left the house. He knew without a doubt that the place would be spotless when he returned, and the smells a lingering reminder to not do his business at home again would be gone as well. Grinning, he went to see about some of the shipments he had coming in.

Chapter 7

Kylie paced her house, knowing that she needed to pack. Glaring at the piles of her things around the room, she wondered how on earth she'd gathered so much stuff in such a short amount of time. The boxes seemed to mock her as she thought about the conversation she'd had with Daniel yesterday.

"Well? Do you love him or not? Because I'm reasonably sure that he's loved you longer than you have me." She'd looked at him in shock, but said nothing. "I know that he's leaving tomorrow to give me the opportunity to settle down and marry you. But you no longer want that, do you?"

When she finally found her voice, it was husky and hurt. "I don't know what you're talking about. I'd been infatuated with you...a childhood crush, but love you..." She didn't continue because she found that what she was saying was true. She didn't love Daniel. She'd only been madly in love with the thought of loving him. His knowing grin had pissed her off.

"So you do love him. It's a good thing too. I would hate to see you two mess up what could be a good relationship over some old crush." He stood then and came toward her. "So, when do you tell him? Or are you going to let him go to Paris and live in misery?"

She'd thought about it. More than she'd wanted to. More, probably, than she thought Curtis would have, but in the end, she'd left Daniel and come here. To her house that was set to be foreclosed on in a few days.

She thought about her childhood living with the Hunters across the street. While they'd been growing up, Daniel had been the one who would talk to her while Curtis would stare at her. He'd been sweet, she remembered, but nothing like his brothers. He'd been sweet and all, but not her Daniel. But she kept drifting back to the bank and what she'd learned.

She'd gotten a lot of information when she'd gone to the bank this morning. Not only was the house in the company name, but it too had been mortgaged several times over. Her dad, it seemed, had gone to two banks at the same time and had asked for and received a loan against it. She owed more on the house than the house was currently worth. She could in no way fix this. Not that she wanted to try.

Then there were the credit cards. All of them had been closed, of course, but the amount on them, paper for the printers, ink, business luncheons, as well as a plethora of other things needed to run a large paper. She had looked at the staggering amount and cried. The banker, a new person she'd never dealt with before, had left her in his office to "compose" herself. Like that was even going to be a possibility now.

She looked at the front door when the bell chimed. The car dealership had delivered her car back to her an hour ago without a word. She'd been handed the title and the keys, and he left. She wondered if she should have told him to take it back, but by the time she'd thought of it, he was gone. They had repossessed it while she'd been having lunch with Daniel yesterday just as she'd thought they would.

She looked out the small window on the side of the door and didn't recognize the man standing there. She was about to tell him to go away; she was busy when he knocked hard on the wood.

"Miss Washington, it's Eric Howe. We spoke the other day. I wanted to talk to you about the newspaper and see if you'd reconsider selling it to the other group. I have a sentimental attachment to it and really wanted to speak to you."

She saw his smile and knew he'd seen her. But she didn't trust him. There was something…well, creepy about him. And his smile, it looked like he had been practicing it for years and had perfected it to be friendly. She could see where it might work on some, but not her. She didn't open the door but spoke to him through it. "I told you the other day that it's over with, Mr. Howe. I've already signed the papers, and the new owners will take it over as soon as the papers are filed." The change on his face was quick and furious. She felt herself back away from the window, suddenly afraid. "You need to leave now."

She watched him stretch his neck muscles as if to try and control his anger. She wondered if he thought she was stupid and decided that he more than likely did. He was also a man who was used to getting what it wanted no matter what.

"Could you please give me the name…why don't you let me in? This is just silly talking through the door like this. We could have this conversation sitting down and enjoying a cup of coffee or tea. I assure you that you can trust me." The smile was back, but as before, it didn't reach his eyes. Kylie reached for the umbrella she had in the stand next to the door. "Maybe we can work out a deal between us that will be helpful and fulfilling to everyone."

She was sure that the only one going to benefit was him, and she wasn't going to be happy with the results. "I've said all I want to say to you, Mr. Howe. It's time for you to leave. I will call the police."

He stood there for several minutes, and, just as she was about to pull out her cell phone, he nodded and backed away. When he turned back, her breath caught. Now here was the real Eric Howe, one to be terrified of, and, if he wanted her to be, she would be dead in a heartbeat.

"This isn't over, Miss Washington." He moved his jacket, and she saw the gun. "I'll get the building one way or the other."

She sat down on the couch when he pulled out of her driveway. She knew he'd be back, and the next time, he wouldn't be so polite. She had a sudden urge to call Curtis and nearly screamed when her doorbell rang again.

"I said to go away, or I'd call the police. I told you once already," she yelled from the couch, "that I'm not going to be able to sell to you. Go the fuck away."

"Kylie?"

She whimpered when she heard the voice on the other side and ran to open it. Curtis. She had no idea how she ended up in his arms, but they were suddenly around her, and she was safe. Safe for now, at least.

"I thought it was…I didn't…" She took a deep breath and looked up at him. "Hold me, please."

He did. He pulled her into his body as well as his arms. She did feel safe. She'd never felt so secure in her life, and she looked up into his eyes again. When he opened his mouth, she knew that whatever he was going to ask wasn't going to be anything she wanted to talk about, so she covered his with her own.

His moan nearly had her melt. His body hardened against hers, and she felt his cock swell. Wrapping herself around him, she moaned when he lifted her ass up, and she was able to hold onto him while he took over their kiss. And when he did, nothing else mattered.

"Kylie, I want you. Please tell me that you want me as well." She wanted him now and forever but would take what she could and kissed him again. "Bedroom?"

She pointed to the couch, and he shook his head. Her bedroom was a mess, but the spare only had boxes. She pointed the way to the end of the hall, and he took them both toward it. All the while, his hands were making short work of removing her shirt.

By the time they reached the bed, her blouse was off, and her bra was opened. Curtis was suckling at her nipple as he took them to the mattress.

~~~

Curtis' mind was a whirl of activity. Her taste made him think of things he'd never dreamed, her warmth made his mind fuzzy, and her sounds, the small sounds of pleasure, made him harder than he'd ever been. But when she wrapped her legs around his waist when they made it to the bed, all he could think of was *mine.*

There were no words between them now. Need had taken over his body, and he was going to give her all he was. His heart already belonged to her, and now it seemed his body would also. Never had he ever wanted a woman like he did this one.

Pulling from her, she whimpered, and he nearly returned to her. But he wanted to look at her this time, wanted to see her beautiful body and savor it. He kneeled next to the bed and unsnapped her jeans. He watched her face as he moved the zipper down the teeth.

"I'm going to enjoy fucking you. But I want to taste you again. I want to feel you come in my mouth again." He stood and pulled her jeans off as well as her panties. Her panting breaths made her breasts sway, and he reached down and took the hardened peak into his mouth. Letting it go with a pop, he licked the abused area and stood over her nakedness.

"Please. I want you."

He nodded at her. But he wasn't going to be rushed, not this time.

"Curtis, please. I need to feel you inside of me."

"I will be soon enough. I want to lick you all over." He took off his shirt and tossed it toward where he'd thrown her clothes, then his pants and boxers. He stood before her hard and naked. "But I plan to take my time."

Settling on his knees again at the bottom of the bed, he put her legs on either side of his hips. She was beautifully trimmed, and he could see her wetness as it dripped from her curls. His cock ached to be inside of her; pre-cum dripped from his head, and he ran his thumb over the swollen member. When she took his hand into hers. He nearly came when she took his thumb to her mouth and suckled it clean.

"Christ." He wasn't going to get his wish. "I'm going to make you pay for this, love. You're going to get the fucking of your life."

Leaning forward and holding onto his cock, he rubbed it into her cream and moaned when she tried to bring him into her. This was going to be much faster than he'd wanted, but to have her beneath him was more than he'd ever dreamed. Taking her mouth again, he slid into her heat and stilled.

She'd been a virgin, and he'd just taken it without thought.

"Baby, be still. Please. If you continued to move like that, I'm not going to be able to be gentle." He rocked into her again when she dug her nails into his arms.

"Don't stop. Curtis, if you stop now, I'm going to hurt you." He moved into her again and watched her face. There was only pleasure there, and he moved again. "Please, more. I need more."

He reached behind her and grabbed her ass. If she wanted more, who was he to say no? Sliding his fingers down her ass, he held her to him as he pounded into her. She'd be sore tomorrow, but he wanted her too badly now to be gentle any longer. When she screamed out his name, he nearly joined her, but he wasn't finished yet.

Her face was beautiful while she came. She was lovely anyway, but her face in complete rapture was one he'd never forget. Sliding his fingers into her tight hole, he watched for any sign that he was hurting her and smiled when she moaned again.

"You like that, don't you?" She nodded and gripped his shoulders as he slid deeper with long, slow strokes. "Your sheath is tight around me, Kylie, like it was meant to be wrapped around my cock."

"More."

He chuckled at her. She was a greedy little thing, and he leaned down and kissed her quickly on her mouth. Then he made his way to her pert nipple and took only the tip into his mouth.

"Curtis, please."

"Please what?" he asked her as he stopped moving. "Please nibble at your nipple again? Please fuck you until you can't walk? I would love to do both those things to you, but you need to come again for me." He moved slowly again and watched her face tighten. "You want to come, don't you, baby? Come for me, and I'll fill you with my cum."

Her body bowed beneath his, and he felt her climax as her channel milked him. His balls seemed to fill instantly and then spew forward. His own climax ripped from him as he threw back his head. Christ, it felt as if he was coming with his entire body.

He rocked into her tight. His cock felt fused to her, and he thought it the best feeling in the world. When he felt as if he'd been drained of every drop of energy, he dropped down onto her and then rolled them to his back. Her body draped limply over his. He hoped to Christ the house didn't catch on fire; he was a dead man if it did. There was no way in the world he was moving anytime soon. When she stirred, he reached for the side of the blanket, pulled it over them both, and closed his eyes.

He needed to talk to her, ask her about whomever it was she'd been telling to go away, but not now. He wanted to bask in the relaxed feeling of being sated. Sated with the one woman he'd never thought to have. He thought about Daniel for all of a second and decided that he'd deal with him later. He was simply too happy right now to care.

When he woke, she was gone. He looked around the room and noticed that she'd folded his clothes and put them over a chair. He stretched hugely then reached for his pants. He found he wanted her again and decided that he'd see if she wanted to shower too. He'd have to be gentle this time… if she let him. She'd be sore from their lovemaking, and he didn't want to hurt her more. He was nearly down the stairs when he saw the note. He was frowning when he picked it up, knowing that it wasn't going to be a heartfelt love letter.

"My father has been hurt. I'm at the hospital with him. Please lock up when you leave. I'll see you around." Then it was signed with a single *K*. He wadded the sheet up and started to toss it away when he decided to keep it. He started for the stairs again when he saw what she'd been up to.

Packing. She was packing up her belongings and from the labels on the boxes, thinking she was sending them out west. Well, not now, she wasn't. He didn't want to think about his own packing and the boxes that now sat at the bottom of his stairs to be put into storage. Nor the call he'd made to the realtor to sell his house. This wasn't the same. He could help her. He raced up the stairs and into her shower. Time was wasting.

The hospital was a hive of activity. There were police everywhere as well as his family. He wondered about that for a second until his mother saw him and came toward him. She engulfed him into her arms.

"I was going over to see if he needed anything else. And there he was all broken on the porch. Who would do such a thing to a poor old man?" She sniffled a little then looked up at him. "She's a mess. I don't know what to tell her. She keeps saying she's sorry to him."

Sorry? He knew that she'd not had anything to do with her dad being hurt, but he did think about the person she'd been trying to get rid of when he'd shown up. He kissed his mom's cheek and went to find out where Kylie had gone.

He found her in a room all alone. He didn't think she'd heard him come in until she spoke. And when she did, he didn't know if he wanted to pick her up and hold her or bend her over his knees and bust her ass.

"I know we had a deal, but I can't sell you the newspaper. I will have to...I need to break our contract." He watched her stare off into the room and turn her cell phone in her hands. "I'm really sorry about that, but I have to do this."

He moved into the room and closed the door behind him. He thought about turning the small lock, but didn't, and moved to kneel in front of her. He brushed the tears from her cheeks and took her phone from her. He put it into his pocket to see later who, if anyone, had called her.

"Who is threatening you, sweetheart?" He wasn't surprised when she didn't answer, but he wasn't giving up. "I can't let you out of the contract, Kylie. Nor can I help you if you don't tell me who hurt your dad."

She looked at him then away again. He could see the fear in her eyes and hoped that whatever happened, he could help her with. If he knew his family as well as he did, they'd want to be there for her as well.

"I don't know what you mean. And I need to break it if only to see if I can pull...do this on my own. I'm not without resources, you know." He heard the bite in her voice and knew if he grinned at her, she'd knock him on his ass. "The Hunters aren't the only game in town."

"No. But I have already filed the paperwork, and as of you leaving my office yesterday, I own the building, not the Hunter Corporation." She looked at him and stood quickly, nearly knocking him over. "Kylie?"

"Will it say that? That you own the building and not the Corporation?" Before he could answer her, she continued. "If that's what it says, then he'll come for you next. Not just the Hunter Company, but you, the man. What the hell were you thinking to take on...you're going to get yourself killed, you know that?"

He knew just when she figured out she'd been talking out loud. The look of horror on her face was telling, and he stood up to pull her into his arms. When she backed away, he had to take several breaths before he spoke without thinking.

"I'm not going to let anything happen to you. Nor to your dad anymore. You have to tell me what he said, what he threatened you with so that I can help you." She started shaking her head before he finished. "You can't think I'm going to let you do this on your own now."

"Nothing has changed. We…we can't see each other any…we can't be anything to each other. And he told me to keep my mouth shut, or he'd kill him next time. As it is now, he's going to be…I don't have the money for this." She broke down, and he was able to hold her finally. "I don't want my father hurt. I don't want to move away. What am I supposed to do with a house that's worth two hundred thousand that has a mortgage of over five hundred thousand? He's going to kill us both."

Her sobbing nearly broke his heart, but he held her. When she sagged against him, he picked her up and held her in his arms as he sat in the chair she'd been in. He pulled out his own cell phone after she'd fallen asleep and called his brother.

"I'm in the last office at the end of the hall near the entrance. I have something I need for you to do." He looked down at her when she stirred and lowered his voice more. "I also need for you to put someone in front to watch over Mr. Washington."

"Do you know who hurt him?" He grinned at Jesse's question and the excitement in his voice. "And do I get to play with the big boys?"

"Yes. I have a phone I need you to look at. Also, her dad's phone. See if there are any matches to any on hers. I have a feeling that he's called her since she came here, so it might be easy for hers. Her dad's phone might be trickier."

Jesse snorted. "Maybe for some, but not me. I'm nearly there. Am I walking in on something that's going to scar me for life?"

"No. And be quiet. She's asleep and going to be mad enough at me if she finds out I'm not taking no for an answer." As he closed his own phone, he thought he heard Jesse laugh, but wasn't sure. He opened the door a few seconds later.

After Jesse took the phone and left, Curtis took her over to the small couch and laid her down. She wasn't heavy, but he needed to use his hands to look some things up. Pulling out his phone again, he signed onto the network and began looking into all the information he could about the *Washington News*. There had to be something there.

Chapter 8

Eric was nursing the bruise on his hand when Mary came in. She was fussing about something, and he found that he was about to pull his gun out and use it on her when she said something that caught his attention.

"What did you say?"

She looked up from the pillow she was fluffing when he asked her again.

"Did you say that someone named Hunter bought the building?"

"Yes. My friend Lily said that he purchased it for a lot more than she thought it was worth, but that's the rich for you. She said that a single Hunter, not the Corporation, owned it now. They'd already started moving things out when the ink was barely dry on the deed. Got himself a deal on the taxes, too, because he plans to make it a business that'll hire a few more people."

She still had the pillow in her hands when she sat down. He got up to pace and realized that the pain in his hand had worsened rather than abated. He took another five pain relievers and drank down a large gulp of bourbon. Her tisking at him nearly had him snarl.

"I need you to find me a doctor that'll come here and not ask any questions. And he'd better know that when he leaves here, he'd better have a poor memory of what he did." He took out an envelope of cash he always had in the drawer to use. "Call that friend of yours and see what she can find out about the Hunters' purchase. I want to know just who bought it and how much they paid for it."

She got up to take it from him and stopped on her way to the door. "His name is Curtis, Curtis Hunter. He's one of the older men that own nearly all the businesses in town. They seem to be a nice enough bunch of young boys if not a little too beefy for my tastes."

She slipped out the door to leave him wondering what she'd meant by beefy. He looked down at his hand and wondered if he'd broken it.

The old man had been a little pissy with him when he'd called him earlier today. Washington had told him that things were looking up and that he need not call them anymore.

"Where is that daughter of yours?" Eric had asked him. He had begun to think he could make her do what he wanted by simply bullying her. "I want you to put her on the line right now so she and I can get this settled."

"She's not here, and you leave her alone. That girl is mine, and you'd be smart to leave what's mine alone." That from a man who was in the crapper because he couldn't run a damned business had made Eric see red. "You stop calling here, or I'm going to have my number changed and have you arrested. I have your name, you…you mean person. Stop calling here." Then he'd slammed the phone down.

Eric still had the ringing in his ears when he went out to get into his car. He'd never had anyone slam a phone down before and had barely known what the term meant. He did now and was going to make the shitty asshole pay for it. By the time he'd gotten to the house, he'd been spoiling for a fight, and being met at the door with a rifle had startled him into a temper. Jerking it out of his hands, Eric hit him with it, and Washington tumbled to the porch.

The man had been about to be dead when Eric heard someone behind him shouting. He didn't realize it was for a dog and not him until he'd been about half a block away. He nearly turned and went back to finish the job when he saw someone pull into the old man's driveway and get out. He didn't stick around after that, knowing the police would be pretty close behind.

And now he was afraid he'd left a bit of his DNA behind. The stupid man had bitten him. And hard too. The skin was broken, and Eric couldn't remember if he'd dripped any anywhere while he'd been there. He was reasonably sure he hadn't, but now that he knew the Hunters were involved, he was no longer so sure.

The older Hunter had been a thorn in his dad's side for years. Eric wasn't sure what the man had done to his father, but it had been enough to have his dad snarl at anyone that even mentioned the Hunter name. Hell, he wouldn't even go hunting.

Eric went to pull out the large notebook his father had had in his desk that day. He'd never really looked in it, not caring who did what to whom or when it was done. He looked now to see what he could find on the Hunters.

He'd found it after several hours of work. His father's handwriting was scribbles at best, and his spelling atrocious. It took him nearly twenty minutes to figure out that "rubbed" was actually robbed and that "dollard" was dollars. His father had hated a man he thought had taken eight dollars from him in a poker game. A game that his father, the idiot, hadn't even been sure of who had been there playing with him.

Moron. His father had been a moron. Never mind that he couldn't hold onto his own money, but to accuse someone else of taking it too was idiotic. He tossed the book onto the table to have it slip off the edge and hit the floor. Several sheets of paper fell out, and he was stuffing them back into the thing when he noticed something else. Something written in much neater handwriting than his father's would ever hope to be.

"The Biloxi building was never owned by the family. It was owned by the organization. When we go and get the money, we have to be quiet about it. If the organization finds out about it, they will take it all." The note was signed by *"M."*

He turned it over several times, hoping for more information. Then he tried to remember if he'd seen any "M"s in the notebook itself. Nothing. He looked over the other two sheets of paper and found that one was a receipt for some jewelry, and the other was a claim ticket to a locker in the bus station. The now closed down bus station.

Eric put the locker claim ticket in his pocket and the notebook in the bottom drawer. There was a knock at the door that startled him and, when he bumped his sore hand against the desk, he let out a stream of curses that would have made even the worst criminal blush. He snarled for whoever it was to come the fuck in.

"The doctor is here. He is in the hallway. Is it all right to send him in?"

Eric looked at her like he'd never seen her before. When she repeated what she'd said, he nodded. Could she be "M"? He knew she'd been around for a long time, but could she be? He started to search for something she might have given him.

A note or a list. He couldn't remember her giving him even a card for his birthday, but he searched anyway. When the doctor and she came back in, he asked her to write up a list of things that he needed. When she raised her brow at him, he told her his hand hurt. She wrote out the list of things as they popped into his head. Dry cleaning to be picked up, shirts to be bought, and something to organize for the next time he went to New York.

He couldn't think of every letter that was written, but he had come up with a lot of them. The doctor left him with a wrap and a prescription, and as soon as he left, he sent Mary on her way. He was disappointed to see that nothing even came close to what he had to compare it to. "M" was not his Mary.

~~~

Kylie woke scared. She didn't know where she was, nor did she have any idea how she'd gotten here. She nearly fell over the lump lying next to her. Would have too if he hadn't grabbed her to keep her from hitting the floor. As it was, he lowered her to where he was on the floor beside her.

"Damn, girl, but you're noisy when you wake up. Let me catch my breath, and I'll turn on the light." She felt his body move, shift near her. She wanted to reach out and touch him but fisted her hands so she wouldn't. "Are you all right?"

"Yes. Where are we?" When he'd whispered, so did she. He moved to face her. She could feel his breath on her face when it suddenly hit her that she'd been seeing to her dad. "My father."

"Hush, he's asleep. I think so, anyway. They said so long as you didn't disturb him, you and I could stay in here. But if you keep squealing like a cat in a room of rockers, then they might change their mind."

She jerked away from him, only to be brought back to his warmth. "I do not squeal." She pinched his arm. "And I do not appreciate you making arrangements without my consent. Who do you think you are anyway? My keeper?"

She got up quietly and moved to the bed. She looked down at her father and hurt for the bruising on his forehead and the stitches she knew to be under the gauze. He'd been hurt because of the stupid building, and she wanted this whole thing to be over with. Kissing his cheek gently, she stepped over Curtis to sit down on the couch. But he pulled her down onto the blankets that he laid on. She realized there was a small cot under him, as well.

"You need a keeper sometimes, I think. He's going to be fine, Kylie. He's getting the best care." He moved her over his body, and she straddled her legs over his hips. When she started to move off him, she felt his hard cock beneath her. His moan confirmed what his body was telling her.

There was enough light in the room for her to see that he'd taken off his shirt. She ran her fingers up his arms to his elbows and then under his t-shirt. She remembered the tattoos there from when they'd had sex and touched them now. "Is this why you wear long sleeve shirts all the time?" He nodded. "I would show them off to everyone if I had one. Of course, I don't have the arms that you do, so mine would have to be much smaller."

"I've had them for nearly ten years. Sometimes I forget that I even have them." She watched his eyes close when she moved the short sleeve up to see them. "They hurt like hell when I had them done. I was nearly drunk out of my mind by the time he'd finished both arms. I had to go back several times to get them finished up. I only had the barest of ink on when I sobered up the first time."

She'd bet he would have had to have been. They reached from the shoulder to his elbows with a different one on either arm. She looked at them closely and wondered what they were.

He laughed and told her that he hadn't known at the time, but had had to look them up. "The one on my right arm is a tribal. Well, they both are, but the center of the one on my right is the fraternity that I belonged to. See?" He moved the sleeve up and traced the dark lines within the long, sharp, knife-looking ink. "The other is a black widow spider and her web. I have no idea why I picked that one. I'm terrified of spiders."

She looked at his face to see if he was serious and realized he was. Big, strong Curtis Hunter was afraid of spiders. She grinned at him before leaning down and kissing the beautiful arachnid.

"I love them. The way they make something so beautiful out of nothing. Did you know that spiders can make as many as twenty webs in their lifetime? And those can withstand so much." She kissed his shoulder and licked at the pounding pulse at his throat. "They also can lay up to thirty thousand eggs at a time." He shivered, and she sat up.

"I don't want to be rude, but do you think we could change the subject? I'm having a hard time concentrating on your words." His voice was husky and deep. She could feel it move over her skin like he was touching her. "Come down here and kiss me. I find that much sexier than spiders and webs."

She leaned down to give him his kiss when he wrapped his hands around her waist. Before she could figure out what he was doing, he starting rubbing her up and down his thick shaft. His mouth under hers was the only thing that kept her from begging him to take her now.

When he rolled her to her back, and he settled between her thighs, she moaned. His mouth moved along her jaw and to her throat until she could hardly breathe past the pleasure. He was making her want him in the most delicious ways.

He moved back up to her mouth and gentled the kiss. He was breathing as hard as she was, and his cock felt good against her. He leaned up on his elbow and looked down at her. "As much as I'd like to finish this, I don't think now is the time. Not only could we be interrupted, but we would more than likely be extremely sore tomorrow." He kissed her nose and smiled. "You're going to hate me when I tell you what I've done, and I'd rather use sex to have you like me again."

She didn't like the sound of that and frowned up at him when he prevented her from sitting up. "What have you done? And don't tell me that you've done it for my own good or, so help me, I'll brain you."

"For the record, I wouldn't have had to if you didn't keep secrets from me. We'll take care of that when we marry. Husbands and wives shouldn't keep — what the hell was that for?" She started to pinch him again, and he stopped her by grabbing her hand. "Behave, or I'll spank you. Not that I don't think that would be fun, but we have to talk."

She heard the door open behind her, and a blanket was suddenly over her. He talked with the nurse as she told him what her dad's blood pressure was, and he also told her that she'd gone to the bathroom. The nurse asked if he needed anything; then, when he said no thanks, the blanket was pulled off her.

"Why did you do that? It's my father, not yours." He nodded down to her chest, and she flushed hotly to see that not only was her blouse open, but her breasts were exposed.

"I can't believe…how did you do that?"

"I'm that good. And you were that tempting." He sighed heavily when she did up the last button. "We have to talk. What do you know about the man who's been calling your father?"

The question, so out of the blue, took her a minute to think about. Before she could censor her words, she blurted out what she thought of him. "His name is Eric Howe. And before you ask, no, I don't think that's his real name. I've never actually met him, but he has a real hard-on for the newspaper."

He kissed her nose again. "Please don't talk about hard-ons at the moment. Mine is about to make me hurt." She giggled, and he swatted her ass. "I said to behave. Now, where were we? Oh yes, Howe. He's not the real Eric Howe. He died in nineteen eighty-two. We have a DNA sample that Jesse is working on. Your father hit him, we think. There was blood in his shirt and on the butt of the gun."

She looked over his shoulder at the bed. Curtis assured her that he was fine, and she nodded. He'd been so pale when she'd seen him, and now… "I don't think he's going to give up. Howe, I mean. There's something about the building he wants. I don't think it's the paper, but the actual building."

"Why? What did he say that made you think…when did you speak to him? The phone call he made to you here, or has he called you at home?"

She glared up at him. "I'm not even going to ask you how you knew he called me here. But you pull any more crap on me like that, and I'll be the one that is spanking you." He moaned, and she had to keep a straight face at the pain she saw there. "He came to my house. And no, I didn't let him in. He was pretty polite until I told him that I'd call the police if he didn't leave."

"That's when I showed up." She nodded again. "The number he used to call your phone and your father's is a cell. And the person it's registered to is dead as well. I'm betting he killed them for the phone, and he took it from his or her body, or he lifted it from someone. Either way, it's hard to trace. Not impossible, but hard all the same."

"I started to do a...wait a minute. I'm not marrying you. I've got a plane ticket to go back to California in a few days. Besides, I don't even like you. And you most assuredly don't like me."

"No. No, I don't. I love you." She looked to see who he was talking about, and he pulled her chin to his. "I have loved you nearly all my life. And I've already talked to Daniel, and he said you love me as well."

"He didn't tell you the truth. I don't...I've been in love with him...with Daniel. And I'm not going to...what are you doing now?" He sat up and reached into his coat pocket before lying back down beside her. "Curtis, you have to know that we can't suit. We have different things we want out of life, things—"

"Do you want to be happy, Kylie?" She nodded. "I want you to be happy as well. Do you want to be with someone that you could love forever?" She nodded again and started to speak, but he put his hand over her mouth. "I'm not finished. I want you to be happy at all costs. I want to keep you safe and warm. I love you, Kylie Washington, and have since the first time I had you beneath me."

"Curtis, even you know that you can't love someone that fast. We only had sex a few days ago. It's just that you're needy, and I'm here." He kissed her long and hard and left her breathless. "That was nice."

He laughed. "The first time I had you beneath me was

when you decided to play football with us. Remember? It was a cold fall day, and you'd been watching us...well, watching Daniel, from your porch. When we decided to even up the sides when Jesse went into the house, you came over and tried to play. I tackled you and gave you a concussion. Your father was pissed, hell, my mother was livid for a week, and you had a shiner and stitches in your lower lip." He pulled the scarred area into his mouth and nipped. "I've wanted to do that for years."

She closed her eyes when he continued a path down to her neck. By the time he had her blouse open again, she was wrapping her fingers into his hair. Need coiled in her belly, and she wanted him to take her now. As soon as his hot mouth took her nipple, she arched up to him and held him to her.

"Kylie, I can't take you here, but I can give you what you need." She nodded. Anything to ease the ache in her body. "You'll have to be quiet, love. When you come, you have a tendency to scream. If you do that, we'll get caught. Can you keep it down to a dull roar?"

"Yes. Please, Curtis. I hurt with need." He moved his hand down her waist to the top of her jeans. When he slid his fingers under the band, she moaned deep and nearly came up off the mattress when he opened the button.

"Quiet now. This is going to be fast because if I take too much time, I'm going to get naked and slide my cock deep into your heat." His fingers moved to her panties, and she widened her legs. "That's it, baby. Let me touch you."

As soon as he moved into her folds, she knew that she wasn't going to last much longer. Riding his hand as his mouth took her breast, she had to bite her hand to keep quiet. This was much harder than she'd thought it would be. As he worried her clit and her nipple, she reached for him. A slight brush against his cock made him moan.

"Don't, love." His voice was heavy with need. "If you touch me again, I'm going to come in my pants. And as appealing as that sounds right now, everyone in this hospital is going to see what we've been up to." He slid his finger into her, pushed his thumb against her clit, and she came apart. His hand coming down over her mouth made her realize that she was crying out, but she didn't care at this point. Her world was suddenly a bright kaleidoscope of colors and stars. Her last thought before she blacked out was that she loved him.

Chapter 9

Eric read the paper twice. There was nothing about the old man being dead. So, he thought, the woman, whoever she was, had gotten there in time. He had hoped that with her father dead, the woman would sell him the property without a quibble. But it seemed that the plan hadn't worked either. He glared at the note again.

"'M' who?" he asked the paper again. He'd spent most of the night going over every entry in the stupid notebook and hadn't found a single name that began with the letter. Then he'd gone over the book everywhere, binding as well as the pages, to see if there was something hidden within one of them. Still nothing.

Mary walked in at that moment and set his usual tray on the desk. He looked at the note again then at her. What the hell, it was worth a try.

"Who do you know that might have worked with my father? Someone that would have signed their name with the letter 'M'?"

She looked thoughtful as she moved back his chair for him. "You had an aunt Margaret, but she was as dumb as rocks and probably couldn't spell 'M' if her life depended on it. I think she's dead now. Does this person need to be alive?"

"No." He sat down as she uncovered the silver covers. "I kind of hope the person is, but it's not necessary, I suppose."

"There was this woman who had a torrid affair with your grandda. She's dead too, and I think her name was Marilynn. Strange woman. I think she spent a great deal of her short life coked up." He was beginning to think this was a waste of time. "Then, there was your mother. Her name was Michelle. Her parents were…let me see…Micky and Rochelle Barr. She isn't dead, but I think she's in one of those homes for the criminally insane. She tried to kill off your father a few too many times, and he had her committed."

He'd always thought his mother had died during his birth. He asked her where she was now. "Oh, upstate somewhere. I get a card from her caretakers every Christmas. Your daddy, he donated a lot of money to them to keep her quiet. Michelle was reputed to have been feeding information to the Feds by leaving them notes at the library. No one could prove it, but still, it was hard to kill her off if it was true."

Except for his father. It appeared that he knew a bit more than he had told anyone. He looked over at the note and wondered if he had found it and had her committed to avoid whatever fell on her spilling over onto him as well. If he didn't tell the organization the truth, then she'd be committed, and he'd still have the money. The organization would have most assuredly found out about it if it became public about the money.

"Do you know who in the Feds she might have been talking to? Or was it something she made up?" He'd heard from his father that his mother was the biggest liar in the world. She'd tell one on you if you were standing right next to her.

Mary shrugged. "Don't know. Could have been all in her mind. She was something of a crackhead too. Mostly it was to get away from your daddy, but she'd sometimes get high she would leave you to me. Never seen a woman more unsuited at being a mom than her."

He realized then that he didn't even know what she looked like. There were never any pictures around, and the few times that he'd asked his father about her, he'd been hit or sent to his room. He wondered now if her supposedly talking to the Feds had anything to do with it. But if she knew about the money, why didn't anyone go and get it?

"I'd like to find out where she is. If you could get me that information, I'd appreciate it." She nodded and went to the door. "Mary, do you know if there were any other children besides me?"

He didn't know why he'd asked that. He'd been content with being an only child, but something made him ask.

She looked at him as if he'd been very odd, but answered. "You have an older sister and a younger one. Don't know much about them other than they were taken away when your daddy took himself off to prison that first time." She nodded to the books on the wall. "Somewhere in there is an album. Don't know how it'll help you much, but there were some pictures in here at one time. The older one is about forty now and the younger one…I'd say she's about thirty-five or thereabouts."

He sat there in stunned silence. Sisters. He wondered if they were his or his stepsisters. The younger one would more than likely be simply because he'd never seen her. He started to the wall of books and went back to the table. There would be plenty enough time for that later. Right now, he needed to get that building.

He'd called the Hunter Corporation and had asked to speak to Curtis Hunter. He was told that Mr. Hunter was out on an emergency and wasn't expected to be back until tomorrow. Eric wondered if it had anything to do with the Washington bastard, but decided that more than likely not. The girl had handled everything, and the old man was simply a means to an end. He called the local hospital next.

"I'm sorry, sir, but unless you can give me more information than his last name, I can't give you any information on our patients." She sounded as if she had yawned and then continued. "You'll have to contact a family member and get that information from them. I'm sorry."

The line went dead before he could tell her what he thought of her customer service. She made him feel as if his call wasn't as important as anyone else who had called in, and he felt as if it was. He laid the phone on his desk and fumed about the lack of cooperation he was getting. Picking up the phone again, he made another call. This one, he was sure, would get results.

"I need someone removed. As soon as possible, if not before." The voice at the other end simply grunted. "Where do I send what you need?"

"Main Post Office. One hour." The line went dead, and he laid his phone down. He pulled out an envelope and a sheet of paper. After printing out the information, making sure that he didn't make any of the letters the same, he wiped it down and put it into an envelope. He nearly forgot himself and licked the envelope closed but caught himself. People were so distrusting nowadays. After having Mary take it to the lockbox that only he and one other person had the key to, he decided to go out.

Eric wasn't much of a ladies' man. He wasn't gay by any means, but women, especially women he wasn't sure of, made him feel...well, dirty. When he had a hooker, the only type of woman he ever had sex with, she came to the house and showered using the soap and towels he gave her before he'd even touch her. Then he'd...well, they never told a soul who they'd been with nor where he'd taken them. The back lot of this property was becoming quite the little graveyard. He got into his car to find entertainment for the night.

He had to get that building. His funds were running low, and having to take out Curtis Hunter was going to cost him much more than he thought reasonable. For one thing, the man was worth more than a man had a right to be, and for another, there was the stupid family.

Eric knew who they were. Rich, handsome, and full of themselves. He'd heard that one of them had married poorly and had thought the man a fool. He'd been taught that moving up was the only way to go, and going in any other direction was foolhardy as well as costly. Money is what made the world go around. His phone ringing had him pulling over.

"I found out how much was in the bank. The record filed with the police back then says that there were bearer bonds as well as a great deal of jewelry stolen. Most of the lockboxes were numbered, and it seemed as if the robbers had it down as to which ones to open." That didn't surprise Eric. His father had been very resourceful. "According to the records kept back, then the estimated worth of the jewels is nearly four million at today's prices. The cash another five."

"And the bonds? Are they still worth anything more than the paper they're printed on?" Christ, he hoped so. The rest was going to save his ass, but the bonds could keep him in money for a little longer.

"Oh yeah. Most of them are stocks, from what my resources tell me. And if they're only worth half what he thinks, they could be worth as much as fifty million."

He was glad he'd pulled over. His heart was pounding so hard that he could hear his blood as it raced in his veins. Fifty million dollars. He tried to think of what that might look like and realized how many zeroes that was.

"I see." He tried to sound calm as if this amount of money was something he dealt with daily. "And if not, then how much are we talking?"

Even at half, he was going to be rich; less than that... well, he could live with it, but it wasn't going to be good. He waited for the man to answer, knowing that he was going to try and lowball him so that if it turned out to be untrue, Eric wouldn't take it out on him. Little did he know, he was already a walking dead man.

"Our guess is, at the very minimum, there was close to sixty million in cash and other sundry. At today's prices... you could have very close to two hundred million."

Now that he could live with. He closed the phone when the man started asking questions. Questions he knew were going to piss him off. He'd only used this source once before and, while he'd been happy, he never really trusted him.

So the money was there. Now he had to wait on the man Hunter to be brought to him so that he could ransom him back to his family. That wasn't going to happen, of course, but they didn't have to know that. Smiling for the first time in days, he moved back into traffic and decided to treat himself to two women tonight. Yes, things were looking up.

~~~

"His name is Vaughn LaMancusa. His father, LaMancusa senior, was found murdered a few years back, and we think by his own son." Curtis looked at his brother Royce and then at Kylie. Jesse had brought in the big boys, as he liked to call the Feds when he realized how in over his head they all were. The woman who he'd brought in went on as if she had just told them that she was buying a cake for someone's birthday. "The older one ran a good game, I suppose you could say. He was a bank robber and, until the one that caught him up, he and his crew had never killed anyone. Only robbed banks, then later, he tried his hand at armored trucks. That ended up with him getting another long sentence that he never served because he ended up on the wrong side of a knife. Oh, and he nearly never dealt in drugs."

"Nearly never? What the hell is that supposed to mean?" Jesse flushed at his outburst. "Sorry. I mean, really, what does that mean?"

"We have reason to believe that the son would deal the drugs and claim his dad was behind it. He wasn't. We think that's what the falling out was about that ended in murder. Junior wanted more and more, and Senior was content to keep what he had."

Curtis took the file Agent Pamela Long handed him. He'd thumbed through it already, knowing what most of it said from Jesse. She sat next to Kylie and handed her one as well.

"This is the man that came to the door that day. He said that he wanted to talk to me about the newspaper." Kylie closed the file and looked at him. "I don't think he wants the building. I think there's something more in it."

"Probably." Pamela handed around another sheet of paper, this one a clipping from a newspaper article. "That happened twenty-nine years ago. The robbers were, from what we can piece together, the LaMancusa men. The older, Valentine LaMancusa, Senior's father, middle name John and not Phillip like his son, killed two of the cops and the bank manager. He was the reason that the police arrived like they did. Had they stayed with the plan, we'd still be looking for them."

"Valentine John LaMancusa of the LaMancusa Family?" Royce stood up as he asked. "Christ. That's the family…the LaMancusas used to try and get Dad to work for them. You remember, Curtis, they wanted Dad to be their heavy. Dad never trusted them and always told us to keep clear of them."

Curtis nodded, the memory coming to him now. "Dad worked as a dockworker on the ship lines most nights. He said that he'd hear of a run coming in and would try to get the cops to go and see about arresting them. Of course, no one ever did. Dad said it was because they had the cops in their pockets."

"And they did." Pamela moved to her briefcase, and Curtis went to sit next to Kylie. She'd not said much, and he was worried about her. Pamela started speaking before he could ask Kylie if she was all right. "We got this from someone who ran. She's been in protective custody since she turned herself in. She wasn't very helpful to us at first, but now… well, now that she's dried out, she's very talkative."

Kylie shuddered, and Curtis put his arm around her. She played with the ring he'd put on her finger. It wasn't where he'd put it, but he hadn't officially asked her yet and could live with it being on the wrong hand. For now.

"What does this have to do with my father's building? I mean, the guy wanted it, so we're all assuming that there's something there. What is it?" Kylie looked at Pamela. "You think you know, don't you? You think you know why he's coming after my family."

"The robbery that killed several people, this one." She

pointed to the article. "At the time of this robbery, Valentine owned the building your paper is now in. When they were both arrested, Valentine was only about three blocks from the building. And Senior was coming out of the parking lot. The money from the bank was never found."

"So why haven't you gone in and looked for it?" Royce looked at the agent then at Kylie. "You thought they were in on it?"

"For a while, yes. The other agents thought that soon enough the Washington's, Jon, and his new wife, who had bought the building in a state auction, would 'claim' they found the money and jewels then make a claim for it as if they didn't have anything to do with the robbery. But it looks as if they hadn't. As the years went by and nothing happened, they thought they'd made a mistake. And soon, no one was interested any longer. Not until Jesse came along with the sample we didn't have a match for from a few other murders."

"And now? Now, what do you think?"

Pamela flushed and didn't answer Kylie's question right away. She cleared her throat and smiled. Curtis answered for her.

"Now, we're going to get the shit and have him put away for a very long time." Curtis pulled her into his lap and laughed when she squealed. "And then you and I are going to start our life together."

She looked at him sadly, and he wished he'd not said anything. When she started to rise off his lap, he held her to him. She wasn't going to get off that easily. He didn't pay much attention to the conversation around them, only thinking about the woman in his arms. When the room started to clear out, he held her tighter to him.

"I should go home." She didn't move, and neither did

he. "My father will need me to be there for a little while, but eventually, I'm leaving town."

"Please don't. I want you to stay here with me." He reached for the hand with his ring on it. "I love you, Kylie. I want to marry you." He moved it off her finger, and she balled up her fist. After a few seconds, he was able to get it opened again and slid the ring onto her finger, the correct one this time.

"Do you have any idea how much…of course you know how much money we owe. You know everything about me, don't you?"

He didn't answer because he was sure it was a trap.

"I can't marry you because you feel like you have to make things right for me. I'm a big girl. I can take care of myself."

"I have no doubt that you can. And I'm betting there will be times when you have to take care of me. I'm a huge baby when I'm sick and like to be pampered big time." He kissed her quickly. "I don't care what your finances are. I don't even care if you're worth more than me. And for the record, I will always try to make things right for you. I love you."

"Why? Why do you love me?"

This question he'd been prepared for. He looked at her and told her what had been in his heart since he found out he had one. "I love the way you sparkle when you laugh. The way your mouth curls up when you smile. I love the way you wear jeans and a silk blouse. I love the way you talked to the flowers in your yard when you were a kid, the way you hug. I love the noises you make when you sleep and the ones you make when we make love." He turned her onto his lap and held her face so that he could see into her eyes. "I love you, Kylie Jean Washington. I have loved you with all my heart, and no other woman will ever be able to fill me with such happiness like you do. I want to see you swollen with our child. I want to see you baking cookies for our children's parties. I want to see you when we get so old that we can't see beyond our noses." He rested his forehead onto hers. "I will die without you."

She punched him gently on the arm. "Jerk. How am I supposed to say no to that?" She wiped at her tears, then at his. "Men don't cry. Didn't anyone ever tell you that, bozo?"

"Yes, they do. Real men cry when something they want and need so much wants to walk away." He took her finger again, the one with the ring on it. "Tell me you'll marry me, Kylie. Tell me that you'll make me the happiest man on earth."

"And if you change your mind, you—"

"I won't. Ever. Is that a yes?" She nodded, and he kissed her. Then as he deepened the kiss, he laid her back on the couch and cupped her breast through her bra. The small cough made him growl as he looked up at his brother. "Go away. I'm busy breaking in my future wife."

"I'd love to, but there's a problem. I think someone just tried to break into the Washington building." He looked up at Daniel and frowned. "Of course, you could continue what you're doing, and I can sit here and watch."

"Bastard. Get out. And don't think you won't pay for this. I'm going to love it when you find you someone to love."

Daniel laughed on his way to the door. "Never going to happen, big brother, never in seventy lifetimes. I don't believe in marriage and never will."

Curtis looked down at Kylie and smiled. "I hope it happens to him soon. I so want to rub his nose in it."

Chapter 10

Kylie had asked him to keep it quiet for a few days, but she'd told more people than she'd meant to. First, there was her dad when he woke. They were practically the first words out of her mouth when he opened his eyes. Then the nurse, who brought someone else in to see her ring, and after that, she couldn't seem to keep anything to herself. Especially where the ring had come from.

"It's his grandmother's. She left it to him to give to his true love." She watched the way the light caught in the blue diamonds. "I can't believe that it fit me perfectly. I love it."

And she did too. The blue five carat diamond was in the center of the wide white gold band. And it was surrounded by a dozen white diamonds. The band had a very detailed design with long lines of flowers and hearts all the way around it. It was a ring made for a woman. And she was even more surprised to find that the lettering on the inside of the ring matched their initials exactly. *KJW and CJH* then the year they'd married.

Her dad's laughter had her looking up at him. "You keep looking at it like he's given you the keys to the castle."

He'd told her that the ring was the key to his heart. She flushed when she thought of what else he'd told her it was the key to. The man was very inventive when it came to her body.

They'd made love several times during the night, then again this morning before he'd left for work. She shifted in her chair and glanced at her dad. She needed to talk to him about where she was staying.

"I have to move out of the house. The bank is going to take it any day now, and then I'd have to—"

"You can stay with me. I know a child doesn't want to stay with their parents when they reach a certain age, but I'm sure we can work things out to both our satisfaction." He laughed. "Or did you have someplace else in mind? Maybe a certain young man that you've been working with?"

"I sort of...Curtis has...Dad, it's that I think..." She took a deep breath and let it out. "I'm moving in with Curtis. He said we're getting married soon...though now that I think about it, I don't think he said when. Though knowing him, he's probably got it all planned out right down to the type of dress I'm going to wear. That man can be a bit overwhelming at times when he gets something—"

Her dad's laughter caught her off guard. He was wiping tears from his eyes and smiling so big she did as well. "Oh, darling, you and he are well suited. I'm sure that you'll get the details worked out. I do hope you wait until your old man heals a bit more before you have me walk you down the aisle. I don't want to miss a minute of it."

"You won't. We want you there too. And I'm going to make sure he doesn't make too much out of this. I don't want a big wedding."

"Too bad." She looked up when Curtis and his mom walked into the room. Curtis continued as if Kylie had agreed to what he was saying. "We're going to have a blowout of a wedding, and you're going to be the star. Hello, Mr. Washington. How are you feeling today?"

"Better. Much better. And since we're going to be related soon, don't you think it's about time you called me Jon? I like that better than mister anyway."

Curtis nodded and picked her up. When she ended up on his lap, she tried to get away, and he growled for her to sit. She felt his erection and stilled.

"Jon, I was so worried when I found you." Mrs. Hunter hugged Kylie's dad to her as she continued. "You've no idea what it was like to walk up and find you all bloodied on the porch like that. Whoever did that?"

Kylie looked at Curtis, and he winked and leaned to her ear. "Mom is trying to get him to give details without telling him anything. It will go better for us all if he tells us who did this rather than him hear what we know and go from there."

She understood to a point but didn't want to tax her dad. He'd been hurt badly, and she didn't want him to tire. She was terrified that the man who'd done this to him might return and hurt him again.

"He came right up on the porch like he owned the place. I told him to get off, or I was going to shoot him. 'Course he just knocked it out of my hands. Like it was nothing to him." She watched his face for pain. "He hit me with it. The gun. I don't remember much after that, but that I had to grab onto him. I was told that I got myself a little of the little pisser, and maybe you can figure out who he was. I'm thinking it was that Howe person and he was a mite pissed that we sold to you."

"You never met him before?" When her dad shook his head at her question, she looked at Curtis. "Then how do we know it's the same man I was threatened by?" As soon as the words were out of her mouth, she knew she'd made a mistake. Her dad didn't know about him calling her, and he didn't know that he'd threatened her if she didn't sell. Her dad looked ready to explode.

"Threaten one of mine? You tell me where to find this bastard, and I'll go and teach him a thing or two about manners. The nerve of that little pisser threatening my daughter." He looked ready to climb out of bed, and Mrs. Hunter stopped him.

"And what do you think you can do against a man a third of your age?" She pushed him back to the bed, and Kylie watched in stunned silence as her father did as she told him. "You get out of that bed and, so help me, I will have you tied there."

"You'll do no such thing, woman. What is a man supposed to do when someone threatens his child? Lay here and let him do it? No, sir, he doesn't. I need to find him and—"

"And what?" Curtis grinned as he continued, trying his best to take the sting out of his words, Kylie would bet. "He isn't a good man, sir. He is going to take what he wants from you no matter what he has to do to get it. Including murdering you. Or Kylie. I'm sure that you know that, and that you can't help her if you're about to make yourself weaker. Besides, we want to get married soon, and you being laid up is slowing the process down a bit."

Her dad leaned his head back against the pillow, looking suddenly exhausted. "He already hurt her. And I couldn't do a damned thing about it. It really does make a man feel a hell of a lot older when he can't even protect his little girl."

"You can count on me to keep an eye on her, and Royce and I will let you know what we find out. But only if you get well." Curtis looked at her. "You think you'd mind your dad staying with us a few days? At least until he's—"

"Oh, no. Oh no, I couldn't do that. I can just as easily be at home. Everything is just where I need it. I couldn't do that to you young people." Her dad shook his head and tried to look stern. All she could see was that her daddy was hurt, and she could care for him. "Kylie, tell your young man that I'll be just fine on my own. Any number of the ladies on the street can come see to me."

Kylie nodded and looked at Curtis. "Great idea. I would love that. And Daddy, don't say a word. What if that ass comes back again? What if one of the ladies on your street is there when he does? This is much better. I love the idea."

She smiled when the nurse came in, and she told them that the doctor called and said that her dad could be released. He was so happy he nearly forgot to get dressed and almost left in the hospital gown. He was exhausted again by the time they got him loaded in the SUV that Royce had lent them to take him home.

~~~

Curtis had had the room in the lower part of the house set up before they left. He wanted to keep Jon safe, and having him close and within a house that had the best security was the only way. He lifted the man out of the wheelchair and set him gently on the bed. He was nearly asleep when Curtis moved to go out again.

"Curtis?" He turned to Jon. "You will keep her safe, won't you? I don't know what I'd do without her. She's all I've got."

"I'll keep her safe. And she's not all you have any longer, sir. You have my family as well. The whole lot of them." Jon nodded and lay back down. Curtis was sure he was asleep before he got the door closed.

Kylie was standing in his kitchen. "You use this stuff?"

He nodded and leaned against the doorjamb.

"I don't even know what most of this stuff is for. Like this. What the heck is this thing?"

He quirked a brow at her and walked over by the food processor. Of course, it was the industrial-sized one, and it was stainless steel, but he thought she should have known what it was. He took her into his arms. "I love to cook. And I'm damned good at it. All this stuff I use, but if you don't want it, then we'll move it out and get what you want. But I do reserve the right to have a few things here I that love." She looked up at him, and he could see the stress in her eyes. "I love you, Kylie."

"I love you too. And it's not the kitchen. Though it's very lovely, it's just..." She looked around and then back up at him. "It's so much. And we...we've not really talked about things."

No, they hadn't. And right now, with her body pressed against his, he didn't want to talk now either. He cupped his hand at the back of her head and slowly pulled her mouth to his. She tasted of sweet tea and lemon from where they'd stopped on the way home. Deepening the kiss, he backed her against the counter, and, when she moaned, he lifted her up and sat her on it.

"There are all sorts of things one can do in the kitchen to get it all hot and steamy." He opened her legs and stepped between them. "For instance, we can cook up a nice meal for me. And then I can take you to bed and show you what we can do there."

He realized then that this was their first night together. Truly together. He leaned into her again and took her mouth softly. When she put her hands on his shoulders, he moved his mouth along her throat then to the hollow of her neck. She tasted of paradise.

"What if we skip the heated kitchen and go to bed?" He lifted her shirt over her head as she continued. "It would be so much better up there."

He realized she was worried about her dad. "He's asleep. If you think you can keep from screaming, he won't know a thing." He licked along the curve of her breast that her bra hid from him. "Of course, I might be begging you for release, but that's for later."

She blushed a deep red, and he kissed her again. Showing her how he wanted her to lean back on the counter, he undid her pants and then pulled them off, leaving on her panties and bra. He dropped her jeans on the floor beside her shirt.

"Have I ever told you that I had these counters made just the right height for me? They are just to my hips, see?" He rocked into her and watched her eyes flutter closed. He stopped moving until she opened her eyes. "If you want me to continue with your lesson, then you must pay attention."

"Every time you touch me, my body seems to tremble with need. Every time I think about you touching me, I get so excited it's all I can do not to hunt you down and have my way with you."

He had to move back from her and take several deep breaths. "You have any idea how long I've loved you? How long I've wanted to hear those words spill from your luscious mouth?"

Unclasping the front closure on her bra, he watched her eyes. They darkened, and he could see that though they were green now, they looked almost black. He moved his thumbs under her bra and over her tight nipples.

"Curtis, you're killing me."

He was glad for that. She'd been doing the same to him

since she was a kid.

"Please do something. I need you."

Taking her pert nipple into his mouth, he worried the tip with his teeth. He didn't bite her, though he wanted to, but simply nibbled then suckled her into his mouth. When she moaned again, he moved to take her other breast into his mouth. Going back and forth between the two of them, he licked a path down her belly to her navel.

He suckled on the tiny indentation. His tongue moved into the little crevice until he couldn't think beyond tasting more of her. As he made his way down her thighs, he nipped at her flesh then licked the tiny wound away.

"You taste like something I could feast on forever." He stood up, and she groaned. Moving a chair from the table to where she lay, he sat down. "Of course, I'd be giving up the best part of you."

Her panties were soaked, and she had wet the counter beneath her. Kissing her knee, he felt her muscles tremble and felt a great deal of satisfaction from the fact that he was doing this to her on his own.

Curtis lifted her leg and kissed her calf. "You and I are going to take a bath together sometime soon. I want to wash your entire body, then your hair. Then I want to do this." He took her toes to his mouth and kissed each one before moving up the other leg.

"Curtis," she hissed at him.

He was enjoying himself too much to be rushed now. Besides, once she came, he was pretty sure he was finished. Just smelling her like this was nearly too much. He lifted her leg to his shoulder and moved his hands up her legs.

"I'm going to enjoy this. Every drop of you." He put his hands under her panties, where they tied at her hips. "You should know that I'm going to pay for these."

"Pay for them?" Her voice was husky and heavy. "I don't understand. Why would you pay for—"

He ripped them from her, and she moaned again. Dropping them to the floor, he decided that he was going to start his own collection of her underthings. He knew she'd blush when he told her what he'd done with the other pair. Leaning into her, he licked her inner thigh and moaned. Christ, he was going to die.

Laving his tongue over her clit, he slid his fingers into her. She was so wet that he didn't have any trouble filling her. She was so tight and hot that he felt his cock stretch with need. Suckling her clit hard, he bit her gently and heard her breathing change dramatically.

"Come for me, baby. If you come hard right now, I'll fuck you, then I'll take you to bed." She nodded. Curtis buried his face in her and fucked her with his tongue and his fingers. She came again then again until she begged him to please stop. He couldn't.

Standing, he tore open his pants and freed his aching cock. He was so close to coming that if he only touched her right now, he was gone. Looking at her face, she seemed to realize this and wrapped her legs around his hips.

"Take me. Now. Take me, Curtis." He slammed into her and came. "Yes," she screamed out as he filled her. Grabbing her hips, he pulled her off the counter and took her to the table. Tossing off everything there, he laid her down and took her again. His cock surged forward until he was sure he was touching her womb. Thinking about filling her with his child Curtis took her nipple into his mouth and nipped. A child.

Collapsing on top of her, he felt his legs tremble a little. Leaning up as best he could, he looked down at her lovely face. Moving the sweaty strand of hair from her face, he smiled at her.

"I love you." He kissed her again. "I want you to have a child with me. Soon. I want to see you big with our baby. I want to hold you while she nurses. I want to spend my life having and loving a family with you."

Kylie wrapped her arms loosely around his shoulders and smiled at him. "I'd like that too. But do you think it would be all right if we married first? I don't want to have to be nursing a child while the minister says his spiel."

Laughing, he agreed. Picking her up while she was still wrapped around him, he looked around his normally pristine kitchen. It was a mess. The best kind of mess. Turning off the light, he set the alarm with her still in his arms and started up the stairs. He was nearly to the top when he remembered he was supposed to call his brother when he got home. Since all his things were still in his pants around his hips, he grinned. He thought his brother probably already had guessed why he hadn't called. Life was good.

Chapter 11

The insurance adjuster walked around the building, and Curtis watched him. He'd been dealing with this sort of thing nearly all his adult life. And this guy was a baby compared to the ones he'd dealt with. Curtis had to cover his mouth twice when the man tripped over some of the debris that had been left behind by their would-be robber.

"He certainly made a mess of things, didn't he?" Clarence Baker, the man with the notebook and calculator, wiped ineffectively at the dirt on his pants. "There is dirt everywhere. How was he supposed to find anything with all this…" He waved his dirty hand around the room. "With all this mess?"

"It's equipment, not a mess. They need this to print a daily paper." The man crinkled up his nose, and Curtis looked away to stifle his laughter. "What have you been able to determine?"

Baker pulled out a small notebook. "We would normally say that it's a simple open and shut case, but as the insurance was just paid up the week before after being lapsed for so long…well, we have some questions for the Washingtons."

Curtis had figured this would be his angle. After five

years of the minimum insurance, then suddenly there was a larger policy and paid in advance, he expected this. Didn't like it, but had expected it. He pulled out his phone to call his brother. Curtis owned this building, and as such, it was personal. He called Jesse as his lawyer to come and help him out. He said he was on his way.

"My lawyer is on his way. He will have to be the one you direct your questions to." The man looked panicky. "He's a shark. Perhaps you are aware of him, Jesse Hunter?"

"Jesse? I thought that...my last report said that the Washingtons owned this building." Baker looked at his notes. "When did you say you purchased it and who are you exactly?"

"I'm Curtis Hunter. I've told you that three times. As well as given you a copy of the deed and title. I also told you that the insurance is up to date, as it is on all our buildings. The only reason your company is still on the rider is because Mr. Washington, my future father-in-law, liked you." Curtis took a step toward him. "I, however, do not."

The man took a step back and nearly tripped over a large part of the wall that had been broken during the break in. Curtis looked at the wall again. Whoever had been attempting to break in hadn't had a great deal of time, or they were a novice with the equipment. Curtis was pretty sure it was both.

The wall in question had been knocked down. Luckily, it wasn't a load bearing one, or there would have been a great deal more damage. As it was, all there seemed to be was some loose bricks, a large hole, and dust everywhere. Also, there was the jackhammer as well as a sundry of other tools that made Curtis believe that the guy hadn't had a great deal of knowledge about taking down a wall. He was looking at the hacksaw when his brother walked in. He grinned when he saw the person who came with him. The insurance adjuster was going to wet himself.

"Hello. I'm Jesse Hunter, and this is my mother, Annemarie Hunter. She's here to keep us from knocking you on your butt." Jesse put out his hand, and Baker took another step back. "I'm not going to bite you. Well, not yet at any rate. What seems to be the problem?"

"The firm knows that I'm here. I've told my wife as well… you think this is funny? You've just threatened me." Jesse laughed harder at Baker. "I do not have to be treated this way. I'm here on behalf of the owner and I will not—"

"Then start saying things like 'the policy is up to date, and there will not be a problem with the claim.' Or better yet, 'I'm sorry for your loss, Mr. Hunter, but we will make sure that the claim is expedited for you.'"

"I cannot pay out a claim until I have all my notes." Baker's gaze took in their mother, and she smiled at him. "You understand, don't you. Mrs. Hunter? These things take time. We need to ensure that all parties are—"

"Oh, cut the crap. Either you pay up as your policy says you will, or we sue." She took a step toward him and pointed her finger at him. "You don't want to screw with my family, Mr. Hacker. If you do, then you'll—"

"It's Baker."

She raised a brow at him.

"My name isn't Hacker, it's Baker. I should give you my card."

While he looked for his business card, their mom turned to them with the most incredulous look on her face. As if to say, "Is he for real?" She turned back to him as he held out his card. "I know who you are. And Hacker was something I've always called insurance companies that try their best to take advantage of people." She pushed his hand back at him. "I don't want your card. After today, it won't mean a great deal to anyone. Either do what's right, or you'll need that card to get yourself a lawyer. Do I make myself clear?"

He looked around at the mess again. "Someone broke in, but how do we know that someone from your family didn't—"

"I'd think very hard on that if you plan to finish that statement." Jesse had gone from a relaxed man to a pissed off lawyer in a heartbeat. "Those are defamatory things you're about to spew from your mouth. And I, for one, would love to see the look on your face when you end up in prison for it."

The man didn't have a clue who he was fucking with until that moment. He nodded once then pulled out his phone. The words payout, as well as immediacy, were what they all wanted to hear. As soon as he wrote out the check and handed it to Curtis, he told the man to get off his property. Baker couldn't leave fast enough.

"Did the police get any prints off the equipment?" Curtis shook his head at his mom. "Shame. But I'm betting they can figure out who rented this stuff. The name of the rental company is everywhere."

It was too. *Coleman Large Equipment Rental* was stenciled on the blade of the saw as well. But he told her that wasn't going to help them either. "It had been reported stolen from another job site two days ago. Whoever took it was careful that there were no prints on it. As well as stealing this crap, it doesn't give us a great deal to go on." Curtis tossed the nail gun to the floor. "What was he planning to do? Break the wall down and rebuild it? Does he think we wouldn't notice?"

Jesse laughed. "What he figured on was coming in and breaking into the wall and, *voila*, there was his stash. I wonder if the money is really in here somewhere."

Curtis thought it unlikely. He didn't doubt that the money was somewhere close, but not in here. It had been a very long time, and someone sometime would have come across it at some point. He looked at the wall that had been started on. He thought about the plans that were in his office at home and tried to remember if this was the wall they were taking out to enlarge this area or not. He didn't think it had been.

"Have you thought about using one of those metal detector things? The report said that there were metal locks on the bags they took out."

He shook his head at his mom. "The walls are too thick. And with the brick all around it, the only way we're going to find anything in here is to tear the building down." He stood as he continued. "I'm thinking that this building is worth more to me up than in pieces. If Kylie doesn't want to move back in after we get her and the paper in the new building, then I'll try and convert it into apartments."

His mom looked around, as did Jesse. "I can see that. An apartment on each level would bring in a nice, tidy sum. It would be something that would be good for someone who worked downtown and wanted to live closer."

He moved to the other wall and looked at the bank of windows. The view was perfect too. A perfect angle to see the entire park from here as well as the main street and all the activities that would be going on in the summer months. He looked up when Kylie walked in. And suddenly, everything was perfect.

"The insurance company just called. They said that someone has just canceled the policy on the building. You know anything about that?" She smiled at him, and he grinned back. "They also said that someone from here was threatening one of their employees? What have you been doing, Curtis Hunter?"

"Oh, poop. That man was an idiot. And I called the insurance company before we came inside. Never trust a man who drives a foreign car. My late husband told me that." His mom kissed Kylie's cheek as she pulled her coat around her. "I need to get going now. Come along, Jesse. I have to go to that dinner thing, and I need you to come with me as my date."

"Mom, I told you on the way over, I have—" Their mom simply looked at Jesse, and he sighed. "I guess I have to cancel my plans. See you later, bro, and let me know what plans you have for this thing. I think I know a couple of firms that would give you twice what you have in it right now."

~~~

Kylie walked around the debris on the floor. She was trying to think about how to ask Curtis something and didn't want to sound like she was whining. She looked up at him when he laughed.

"Say it. Or ask it."

She tried to look confused but knew she'd not been able to pull it off.

"You have a terrible poker face. I can read you like a book. What is it, Kylie?"

"I didn't know you were planning to sell it." She flushed. "I know that I don't have any say over it, but—"

"Yes, you do." She looked at him, confused. "You have every right. Or will as soon as we're married. I won't make a decision about our lives without consulting you. If you don't want the building sold, then we won't sell them. The operative word there is *'we.' We'll* own the building, make decisions based on *us,* and *we'll* have whatever comes of it. Understand?"

"But you will own this before we marry. Isn't that the

way the law works?"

He shook his head.

"You would give me half of everything because we're married."

It wasn't a question, but he answered her anyway. "No. I give you everything now. Everything. Because of the fact that I love you, none of this has meaning without you." He walked to her and pulled her into his arms. "What do you think we should do with this if we don't use it for the paper?"

She looked around the spacious room. It had paper equipment, printers that had long since served their purpose but still worked. Binding machines from when they had offered a service to a book dealer to rebind books. There were desks, oak and cherry, that had been scarred over the decades that still stood strong and would for many more to come. She looked at the floors, knotty pine, dulled now by years of feet and printer ink. She looked out the window, the one that faced the pretty park that had been built so many years ago, one that she'd played in as a child. "What would it take to make this a place for children to come?" She looked at him. "A sort of stopping place between the streets and someplace to come for safety and security? We could sort of show them a trade. I don't know, maybe a place where they can learn what all this stuff can be used for."

He looked at her. She had half expected him to laugh at her or to tell her no. "You mean like a shelter. I like it. We could have someone run it, and I know a lot of people who could come here and help out, retired folks with nothing but time on their hands."

She could see that he was warming to the idea. And because of that, so was she. She took out an ever present notebook and started to jot down ideas, people, and things they could do.

By the time it was growing dark, she had filled four pages of notes. And had several more ideas in her head. She and Curtis would make this work, she knew it. It would be a place they could both put their hands deep into. He called his brother Royce and pitched the idea to him. Before they were halfway home, they already had the backing of nine large companies to donate, not only time but the manpower to fix the building up to code and donations. And his mom said she'd make it her priority to get even more money. Things were rolling from a simple idea.

"What do you think it should be called?"

His question startled her out of her thoughts of putting in a small kitchen so that some of the kids could learn to cook if they wanted to.

"It will have to have a name worthy of it. What should it be?"

She didn't have a clue but told him she'd think about it. And her first thought was his father. She had always liked Mr. Hunter and his soft voice and slow ways of getting to his point but didn't know how Curtis would feel about that. So she changed the subject until she could talk to Kasey and the others. "I've been thinking about your house." He laughed as he turned onto the highway toward it. "What if I told you that it's in need of an overhaul?"

"It is. I bought it used and never really got around to fixing the things that it needed. What did you have in mind? Because if it's moving, I'm all for that too." She nearly told him yes, then hell yes.

The house was an older house. Nothing too much about it to recommend them doing much to it. It was a two-story house that sat in the middle of a little lot. She didn't want to go bigger, just...she didn't know, but this house was not what she thought she could raise children in. First off, there was no yard, and there was only a bathroom on each floor. It would never do if they had more than one child.

"Why don't we look around for something so that when we have kids, we'll have a house with a bigger yard and more than one bathroom on each floor?" She thought about the neighborhoods and thought of the one her dad lived on. "There are some houses on Dad's street. We could look there."

He nodded and smiled. She had a feeling he already had a house in mind. She only smiled. She knew that whatever he had picked out, she was going to love it. She thought a smaller three-bedroom house on the street where she'd grown up would be great. And modestly priced as well.

They both were so tired by the time they got to the house that neither of them felt like eating much. After ordering a pizza and eating it, they went up to bed. She was going to go over and supervise the move in the morning, and he had some things to do at the Hunter building. By the time she had showered, she was exhausted and couldn't do more than thank him for having her things brought over from her other house. Yawning hugely, she kissed both her dad and Curtis good night and fell asleep only seconds after her head hit the pillow.

Chapter 12

Eric tried to calm himself. It had been two days, and he was still terrified of what had nearly been the death of him. The fucking place had lit up like a fucking Christmas tree the moment he'd made the first hole. And who fucking knew there was so much more involved in the shit he'd stolen than turning it on and putting it to the wall? He'd been nearly knocked on his ass the moment the thing had been turned on. He glared at the bruise on his arm. And the fucking thing had thrown him against the wall as if he wasn't a grown man.

He moved to the couch to lie down again. His head, where the wall had hit him, was still throbbing. And what did he have to show for it? Nothing, not a fucking thing.

"They're fucking with me, I just know it." He covered his eyes with his arm as he contemplated what he needed to do next. "First, the old man and now his fucking building."

"You should have hired someone to go in and do the grunt work."

He nearly squealed when Mary spoke. He'd been so pissed he'd forgotten he'd asked her to come and see to his arm.

"My old beau used to use a jack when he was a younger man. I could ask him to come and see what he could show you."

"It's too late now. The cocksucker probably already hocked the shit I had to leave behind." She moved the first aid kit to the coffee table and pulled out the scissors. "I don't suppose you have anything for pain in that kit, do you? My head is killing me."

She handed him a bottle of pain reliever and cut away his shirt sleeve. He was going to have to get a whole new wardrobe if this kept up. She tisked at his wound, and he felt himself flush. It wasn't more than a scratch. He was about to pull his arm from her when she turned it over. Now there was a wound that deserved to be pissed about.

"It more than likely could use a few stitches. I can do them, but you're not going to like it overly much."

He nodded and reached for the bejeweled box by the couch and decided that a hit might relax him a bit too.

"You go on doing that shit, and you won't be worth a plugged nickel in a few years."

"You stick to what you know, and I'll do what I do best. I know just when I've hit my limit." He grinned when he thought of that. His dad had said nearly the same thing when it came to his alcohol. He did three lines of coke before he leaned back on the couch. When she touched his arm, he knew that whatever she did to him now would be nothing but pure pleasure.

When he opened his eyes, there was a large piece of gauze on his arm, and the side lamp was burning softly. Mary was nowhere to be seen, and he was feeling the pain from his arm. Looking down at the coke and the mess he'd made, he thought about doing another line just to make it so he'd be able to sleep. As soon as he did it, he laid back.

"Gotta figure out what to do about the building and my money." Yes, he thought, now he could think too. "I've got things that require me to have cash. If I don't, then I'm so fucked."

He had two shipments coming in on Friday, then another one on Saturday. He tried to think what day of the week it was and lifted his arm to check his watch. He was distracted by the way his fingers seemed to be moving and nearly forgot what he'd been looking for. It was Tuesday.

"So, I have three days, give or take to get the money I need. That's not a great deal of time." He pondered that for several minutes, then got up to pace. He nearly fell over from dizziness. "When did you eat last?"

There were no plates on the table he sat at, nor were there any take out bags in the trash. He tried to remember if he'd even eaten today and wasn't sure if he'd eaten yesterday either. He picked up the phone to call Mary and found her note.

"I've been thinking on the 'M' you asked me about. I found your sisters' names. The older one is Martha, and the younger one is Malinda. I know that doesn't help you much."

Not really, but right now, he was feeling too good to let it bother him overly much. He looked around the bookshelves until he found the album. There were places where the pictures had been removed, and he wondered who had done it. He suspected Mary for no other reason than she was the only one there. Grinning, he pulled the album to the desk and started looking through it.

By the time he'd gone through it three times, he realized something. His sisters were as ugly as sin, and he was a fat baby. Tossing it across the room, he watched as a few more pictures fell out. Next time he burned a fire, he was going to use this thing as kindling.

Taking out a sheet of notepaper, he started writing down things he needed to look into. First was his mother. She was alive and well somewhere, and he wanted to find the bitch and see what she was made of. Then his long-lost sisters. Where were they, and how much of his money were they going to want once he found it? None, as a matter of fact. Then there was the missing 'M.' Who the hell was she and how the fuck did she figure in all this? And what organization? Was it the family or some other family?

His phone ringing irritated him, and he picked it up without looking at the ID. He was writing his mother's name when he froze at the sound of the voice on the other end.

"You haven't made this week's payment yet. You want I should come and collect it with interest?"

He slowly laid the pen down and looked around the room.

"You been a bad boy there, Vaughny. You showing up in the police station ain't gonna make the boss happy with you."

"I don't know what you're talking about. I've never been to the police station in my entire life." If one didn't count being arrested, but he doubted that's what the man on the other end was talking about. "Your sources have it all wrong. I've been trying to collect the money that I owe you so we can be square."

"Square?" The man, he never knew his name, laughed. "You know'd we ain't never gonna be square, Vaughny. We be partners. When you got that next load coming in? Soon, I'm thinking."

"Yeah, soon." He rubbed his forehead, forgetting for a moment the bump on the back of his head when he ran his fingers through his hair. "I'm having a big shipment coming in on Sunday."

Eric did have one coming in on Sunday, but it was really tiny compared to the ones he had coming in a few days earlier. He nearly swallowed his tongue when the man on the other end laughed.

"You wouldn't be lying to me, would you, Vaughny? I'm thinking you have something coming in on Friday night. Would my sources be wrong about that?"

His sources. He didn't have a clue who was feeding him information, but he planned to find out. He looked up when Mary walked in. She was the only one that knew besides the morons he had at the docks waiting for it for him. He pulled out his gun and set it across his lap while half listening to the man go on about what happened to liars. He knew what happened, and he planned to take care of that problem right fucking now. He turned his back on Mary when he nearly missed what he'd been saying.

"...tomorrow night. And if you don't show, then there will be parts, important parts of little Vaughny missing."

He nearly asked what the hell he was talking about when he repeated what he'd apparently missed.

"The dock, number one twenty-five at midnight. Understand?"

"Yes. I'll be there. Midnight." He looked around the room. There were suddenly eyes in every corner. He reached for his stash and opened the chest. "Midnight." He put down the phone and looked up at Mary. She had the most bemused look on her face as she held a gun to him. He simply lifted the gun and pointed it at her as well.

"You might want to think that over before you pull that trigger. I've got some answers for you that'll make finding the money and those bonds worth it." She grinned at him. "Besides, you don't want to go on and shoot your granny, do you?"

He nearly put the gun down but waited. She still had hers pointed directly at him. There was something about what she said that made him think she might be telling him the truth. He motioned for her to move over to the table, and she did, never lowering her own weapon.

"Why should I believe you when you say you're my grandmother? All this time and suddenly you come out of the closet? I don't buy it." He moved to the chair and sat down. "What's your angle?"

"No angle. Been waiting for you to show some balls. Or to grow up. Didn't seem to me that you were going to do either." She laid her gun on the table between them and put her hands in her lap. "Of course your daddy and your grandda didn't have the sense God gave a turnip, but there you have it. At least you're trying to make something of yourself."

He nodded, picked up his napkin, and laid his gun near hers. If they were going to kill one another, he figured they'd have done it by now. Instead, he picked up his fork and took a bite of mashed potatoes to his mouth.

When the phone rang again, he ignored it. He was suddenly hungry and sat at the table to enjoy his meal. That struck him as funny, and he was still laughing when the voicemail sound on his cell sounded. Whoever it was could fucking call back. Vaughn Erick LaMancusa was back, and he wasn't fucking around any longer.

~~~

Daniel looked at the woman across from them. She wasn't as worn as he'd been led to believe. Nor did he think she was as spaced out as she was putting on. He leaned on the table and let his brother Jesse continue asking her questions. Michelle LaMancusa, also known as Dawn Stein, was not giving them dick.

"He's alive, you know."

She looked at him then away.

"Your son. I'm pretty sure that by now, he has a pretty good idea that you're alive as well."

"Nope. They told him I was dead. No reason for him to look for his mommy. I'm as good as dead to him." She smiled that far away smile that Daniel knew she had practiced for a very long time. "He's thinking I died while birthing him."

"And Mary Phyllis? She knew, right?" She looked at him sharply then away. He saw it in a second, fear. "She's been around, we know, but not where they are. Probably told him all about you and that girl of yours."

"He won't touch my girl. She's hiding so far from them that nobody will find her." He slid the folder over at her and watched as she tried to ignore it. "What's that? You trying to tell me you know where she is?"

"She's changed her name to Elizabeth Margaret Samuels. She lives in Devil's Island, Washington, and has for nearly ten years. Her foster parents died a few years back, and she was left enough money to start new. She's just been in to visit you last month." Daniel moved the folder closer to her. "You should see what she's done to the house. It's very nice."

The act fell away. In that second, she went from defiant bitch to concerned mother. Daniel wanted to keep leading her on, but time was running out for them. She took the folder and opened it to the pictures that had been taken just yesterday. And the house was very lovely.

"She doesn't know about the family that I married her into. I tried to keep her out of it for as much as I could. But

Vaughn was trying to get me to pull her in so that he could marry her off to one of the other families. When my husband died, that's when I started talking to the Feds. They hid her away for me, and nobody never could find her." She snorted as she closed the file. "Fat lot of good they did me. The fucking prick still hurt me."

"How?" Jesse asked before Curtis could. "How did he hurt you? By putting you away and out of the reach of the money?"

"Money? He didn't have shit. His daddy had it all back then and wasn't too keen on giving any to his son. When he came to Vaughn about the bank robbery, I told him it was a trap. Never would listen to a thing I said. Then when he was arrested, I had to make ends meet. I had a kid I had to raise."

"So it wasn't your husband's idea to rob the bank?"

She shook her head.

"Then Vaughn senior ran it all."

"No. It was his wife. Mary Salinas LaMancusa was her name. She had them all wrapped around her finger back then. Then when she told Vaughn that I was talking to the Feds, it was all I could do to make sure my little girl wasn't touched. His bastard was gonna turn out like him anyway, so I didn't care. But him being his baby, they told him what they wanted, and I was fucked. You know that the people who stashed me away still send the bitch cards all the time?"

Daniel looked at her as he sat back in his chair. He looked at Jesse and decided that it was now or never. She lit another cigarette with trembling hands. They needed information she might have.

"The bank robbery? Do you know where the money is?" She looked at him, then sat down her smoke and picked up her drink. He let her take a large swallow before continuing.

"There have been several break-ins at the building on Biloxi Street. It is rumored that the money is in the building somewhere."

Laughing, she picked up the cigarette again. "Yeah, it's there. I know just where too. I worked there at the time, and it was my job to make sure when they come to hide it that everything was all neat and tidy for the cops to see."

Daniel was stunned. They all figured that the money *might* have been there, but now they knew. He started to ask her where when she pulled a sheet of paper from a stack next to the table. As she started drawing, she told them what had happened that day.

"Vaughn decided that we was going to take what we felt was his. He said he didn't believe the rumors that were going around about me and the Feds, or so he said, but Mary had proof. 'Course she probably had it all. I wasn't very smart back then. I'd meet them at the fucking FBI building whenever they asked me to come by." She looked up at them suddenly. "There's this book. You should find it. It's got all sorts of names in it. Some of the families are still alive, and you might find it helpful to solve a few hundred murders."

He nodded as she went back to drawing.

"I figured that Vaughn was gonna kill me anyway. Him or his daddy. I was supposed to wait until they showed then I was to get the money out the next week and bring it to the meeting place. But they never made it. They was picked up the same day. I hid it in a different spot than they told me to. I was gonna have running money if I ever got away."

"But you never went back for it either. Why not?" Daniel watched her pause in her drawing and then finished it up.

It was very crude, and it took him a few minutes to figure out she was drawing the inside of the building. It was the second floor, and she even drew in a few of the larger printers that were still housed in there. When she finished, she handed it to him.

"I don't understand this." He did but wanted her to explain. "This looks like any building in the downtown area. You'll have to be more specific."

She took it back and put the address at the bottom of the picture then put a large X near the wall where someone, her son, he supposed, had knocked it down. He looked at her then and was surprised by the tears in her eyes.

"I never loved any of them. Especially not my husband. But I was forced to marry him on account of who I was. My family wasn't big in the crime circuit yet, but Vaughn, my husband, was. And me being a widow was something he liked. Made him think that I would be grateful for him. I wasn't. I didn't want that shit. But I mostly didn't want them to have it either. And after a time…" She shrugged. "After a time, I was too used up to care much for anyone to get it." She pulled a necklace from under her shirt and revealed a small locket. "My daughter was all I had in the world. And he…I ain't never seen my grandkids on account of she being afraid they'll say something to someone. You think that's fair?"

"No." Daniel almost felt sorry for the woman. She'd been as fucked as any of them had been in her situation. He pulled out the picture he'd gotten when he'd had the daughter investigated. It was a picture of the three little kids in the yard, along with a dog.

She started crying almost immediately and held it to her heart. It took him a few seconds to realize that she'd never even seen a picture of the children. When she took off the necklace, he thought she was going to put the pictures in it and couldn't see how that would work with them being so big. But she opened it up and took out a small folded piece of paper and handed it to him.

"This will get you the rest of the information you need, including the primer that makes it so's you can read the code. The safe is in the big house, the one that Vaughn and I lived in until he went to prison. I'm sure that even that son of his didn't know this one. After his dad was put away, I sent away for the instructions on how to change the combination. Never did tell them that I knew it. I didn't trust them Feds and for good reason." She looked at the picture again and put it in her shirt. "You find them people and make 'em pay. I trust you now to do the right thing."

She got up and lay down on the bed. She didn't speak again as he and Jesse moved to the door, taking the drawing with them. They were nearly out when she spoke again.

"I never did drugs until Vaughn tied me down and shot them in me. I was a good girl, and once he got me hooked up on them…well, I never wanted to come back down." She sat up slightly. "You tell that boy that I hope he pays for every crime he committed. Every last one of them."

Curtis looked at his brother in the hall then back at the woman. "I plan on it. He fucked with the wrong family when he messed with mine."

"Good," she said softly as she lay back down. "Good riddance to them all too. Especially to that old bastard Vaughn."

Chapter 13

Kylie looked out the window from the second floor of the building. A woman was directing things down there like she knew just what she was doing. And not one man seemed to mind the fact that she was doing the ordering either. She looked up as the man she'd been introduced to late last night stood beside her.

"My wife. Willow can run a crew into the ground, and they'd still love her." They both watched as a fence was put up around the entire parking lot as well as the building in a matter of minutes. "She'll have this place in lockdown in an hour tops."

Last night it had been decided that a construction crew would come on site today and start the renovation. Most of the "crew" consisted of the Hunter family, but there were a few workers on site as well. One of them was the man standing in front of her. Jared Stone owned Stone Construction. She wondered what else the man did besides love his wife. Willow came into the building, still shouting orders to a man named Conley, and they both came up the stairs as if they were nothing but a ramp. She grinned at her.

"Don't you just love the smell of sawdust in the morning?" Willow Stone said with a smile.

Kylie nodded, not sure what the hell that meant.

"I love my job." she continued as she moved to another room, still telling people what needed to be done.

Mrs. Hunter was dressed in jeans and a large flannel shirt and had on the most ridiculous bandanna she'd ever seen. She was walking around the site in two hundred dollar boots. She'd told Kasey, Royce's wife, that there was no need to not be stylish. They had laughed for ten minutes.

"Well, my dear, are you ready?" Curtis stood just behind her as he asked.

She looked up at Curtis and nodded then shook her head.

"You don't want to know what you've been hiding away for nearly three decades?"

"Not really. But I know that's what we're here for." She glanced over at the man who was simply standing against the wall. "Who is he?"

Curtis looked over at him and then back at her. "He says he's with the Feds. William Trust, as in trust me. His words, not mine. But we can't dig this crap out without having a witness, and he came along. That man over there." He pointed to a man standing next to Daniel. "That man is a friend of Daniel's. His name is Charles Mann. I think they went to school together. He's the main reason we've been able to get this crap going so quickly."

Willow walked to the drawing on the floor and looked around the room. Kylie liked the brass young woman who seemed to be everywhere at once and hoped to get to talk to her soon about an article she was thinking about. Women in jobs that men primarily do. She had a feeling that Wills, as she was called, wouldn't like the title, so she was going to work on that before she called her.

"Okay. As far as I can figure, this is where she said it is. If not, then we'll be a while longer." Wills walked around the thick wall of bricks and then faced it again. "Why is this even here? The specs for this floor say that this wall should be over there about fifteen feet. Even my mutts can see that this isn't a load bearer."

Kylie had heard about Wills' dogs. Two large dogs named Come Here and Damn It, respectively. She said that her nephew had one of their offspring, but she wouldn't tell her what he'd named it. She said that seeing was believing.

The hammer that Conley was holding looked big enough to take down the building, much less a wall. He and Jared stood side-by-side with twin hammers and took several deep breaths. When Jared swung his first at the wall, all it did was make dust fly all over the room. Conley didn't do much more than that. But the third and fourth swings brought some of the bricks down, and by the time they were hitting nearly a dozen each, there was a large hole in the wall. The Fed guy stepped closer as the wall started to crumble.

"You do know that whatever is behind here is going to have to be taken into custody, right?"

She nodded and looked at Daniel. He winked at her.

"There will need to be a listing of what is found as well, matched against the inventory that is claimed to be of taken that day."

"Yes. And if nothing matches, then all of that belongs to Kylie. I know what we're doing here. She and her future husband own the building. They're cooperating fully with this." Daniel glanced over at her before continuing. "You might want to back the fuck up, William. No one here is going to run off with the family jewels." He flushed but didn't apologize. Daniel moved her back when the wall took another hit. "He's just pissy because he was on the case all those years ago and talked the Feds into believing that the money wasn't here. I guess it pays to do some research before jumping to conclusions."

"Do you really think there's going to be anything in there?"

Daniel didn't get to answer because Curtis had hit the wall with his turn, and a big portion of it fell away. The shouts made her think of a sports arena. She looked over the heads and shoulders to see that there were bags, gray with dirt, lying in the debris.

She knew bank bags when she saw them. These were old and dirty, but bank bags nonetheless. They waited while William read off the numbers to one of the men that had come with him. So far, it was a match for each one.

After twenty minutes, it was confirmed that the bags were indeed from the First National Bank of Ohio. Now all they needed to do was figure out what was in them. The key that was supposed to open them wasn't working as well as she'd hoped. She wanted to knock the man out of the way and try it herself when, suddenly, the lock popped loudly in the room. William opened the bag and took a deep breath as he reached inside.

The first thing he pulled out was stacks of cash. It looked to her like it was fifties, but she wasn't sure. She knew that there had been a great deal of money stolen that day, and now it seemed that it had been found. She leaned heavily against the press while he took out more and more money.

"It seems unreal, doesn't it?" Curtis helped her by picking her up and sitting her on the press as he continued to talk softly to her. "I knew it was going to be really here, but now that I see it, it's sort of surreal."

"All that money belongs to those people they robbed." Curtis shook his head.

"They don't get it back?"

"The insurance company that the bank held paid everyone back. The people who had jewelry and polices in the safety deposit boxes filed a claim on what they had in the boxes, and it too was paid to them. This stuff, mostly the money, will go to the insurance company if they're still in business. Daniel is looking into that now."

"And if they're not? What happens then?" She didn't think she was going to like his answer when he grinned at her. "Please tell me that we don't get it? What are we supposed to do with all this? People lost their lives for that. I don't think I want anything to do with it."

"I have an idea of how we can use the money. If we get to claim it, we'll use it to set up your project. The money will go a long way to making your dream come true." He moved to stand in front of her and blocked her view of what was going on. "You have no idea how much I want to take you right here."

She was shocked when she looked up. His entire body seemed to be hard and ready. She leaned her head against his chest and heard his heart pounding. Christ, would she ever be able to get enough of this man? She doubted it. And he'd been right in front of her, her entire life. She wondered when she'd gone from finding him to be the most irritating boy on the planet to the man she wanted to spend the rest of her life with. She found she really wanted to spend her days making him very happy. Starting today.

"You're insane, you know that, right?" She almost didn't recognize her own voice. It had turned rough and low. "There are any number of people in this room who can hear you."

He laughed. "But you're the only one I care about."

His kiss was devastating. His body pressed against hers, and she melted against him. When he pulled back, she was breathing hard and suddenly didn't care about the goings on around them. When he took a step back, she whimpered.

"We have all the information we need. We'll lock this up and take it—" William was cut off by a man standing next to him. The man that Curtis said was a friend of the family.

"This money is going into a vault until such a time as we can determine who it belongs too. You'll get a receipt for it."

Kylie looked at Curtis when he stepped in front of her. Something was going on here.

"You might want to hand that officer your weapon."

She started to jump down, but Curtis held her back. He was covering her, and she was suddenly grateful when the man who'd been counting the money had leaped up. His gun was the last thing she saw before she was thrown to the floor.

Shots were fired. Four if she had to guess. And when she was able to move the heavy body on top of her, she looked around the room. Willow, like her, had been thrown to the floor, and her husband was lying on top of her. Curtis helped her up but didn't let her go near what looked to her like a body. Someone had killed the Fed.

"He wasn't."

She looked at Jesse, just realizing that she'd spoken out loud.

"We weren't sure at first, but it looked like he'd been planted. Charles had a feeling that he wasn't who he said he was all along. He had a gut feeling that he had been a plant and, other than that, we had nothing. But when he broke protocol and wanted to take the money, we had him."

"They don't take the money on things like this?"

Jesse shook his head.

"Then where does it go? Someone has to take it. It can't wait here for Eric to come and get it." She looked at where the money was and noticed that someone was putting it back into the wall. All of it. She looked at Jesse first then at Curtis. Something wasn't right.

"We need to catch LaMancusa. If we pull the money out now, he'll simply get away. If he's not sure, then he'll try again." Curtis nodded when she started to shake her head. "We have to get him off the streets, honey. If we don't, then he may kill others."

But the money was still in the building. A building she and he had plans for. She started to protest again when she saw the man being covered with a sheet. He'd died for this money, and she didn't have a clue as to why. She wondered if she ever would.

"He was in with one of the families around here. Not sure who right now, but it's safe to assume that someone knows about the money besides us." Charlie shook her hand. "You did great. I never would have known that you weren't aware of things going down."

Curtis cleared his throat, and Charlie walked away.

"I was supposed to know. Why? Was it because he wouldn't go along unless everyone knew?"

"Something like that. He said that all parties had to be present and everyone had to know the plan. I was afraid you'd freak out or not let us do this."

She looked over at the dead man and glared at Curtis.

"That was not a part of the plan."

She believed him. She didn't like it but believed him. She started to pace the room as the wall was put back up.

She was beginning to think that there was a great deal she wasn't aware of. When she stopped walking and looked back at Curtis, he was leaning where she'd been, and his arms were crossed over his chest.

"Did you kiss me to distract me?"

He shook his head.

"Then what? What made you want to kiss me right then?"

"I needed it for my own sanity."

She liked that answer but didn't let on.

"And I was terrified that I'd made a mistake by agreeing to have you here. We thought that he might try something, but we weren't sure that he wasn't going to try it here or when he tried to leave."

~~~

Curtis watched her process the information. He loved to watch her face, and when she finally got it, he could see it all over her body. She wasn't any happier, but she did seem to get what had just happened.

"He works for either LaMancusa or some other big crime family. And if it's not the LaMancusas, then it's someone else. If it's someone else and the man was willing to die for them, then we might have bigger fish to fry than we thought."

He nodded as she continued.

"If LaMancusa is aware of what was going on here, then any of the people here would know as—"

"Not anyone here. All these people, including the Fed, are friends of the family and have been for years. Wills and Daniel went to school together. Jared and Royce have been friends forever."

She believed him. She could see the friendship here and wasn't surprised that even Mrs. Hunter was a part of it. Kylie watched as Mrs. Hunter cuffed Jared in the head. She laughed when he did. "What do we do now? We know the money is here. Now, what is the plan?"

He took her to the lower level and showed her around the building she'd been a part of since she was a child. "There are cameras everywhere. I had them installed a few days ago. The boxes that we were using to move out some of the newspaper equipment were actually bringing in the camera equipment. Once the boxes were empty, they loaded them up with the things to move over to the new building. It's been a long project, but things are finally in place. Then after this is over, we'll put them back once the building is up to code."

"And you think he'll try again?" He laughed, and she thought of something. "You're planning on it. You know he'll come back because…because you're going to make some sort of slip about the money."

"Not about the money, but that we're going to go searching for it. Next week. The newspaper is going to run its first online story about it on Friday. Then on Wednesday, we'll come here and take it out again. Only this time, there will be news teams here to cover it."

"You think he'll try and come before then. You think he'll break in again and, this time, find it. Or you'll catch him in the act." He kissed her, and she'd felt as if he'd handed her the keys to the castle. "What if he doesn't come?"

"Oh, he'll be here. It's too much money for him not to. Besides that, we have it from a very reliable source that he needs the money to be able to breathe past Thursday. There is a heavy hitter in town that LaMancusa owes a great deal of money to."

She looked up sharply. "Another Fed." He nodded. "And this Fed? He's a trustworthy type?"

"Yes. It's Charlie. He's been playing this game for a

while now. This, what's going on here? That's going to be his crowning glory. And when it's done?" Curtis took her into his arms. "When this is done, you and I will be married and off on our honeymoon."

She nearly asked him if they could go now, but a large, wooden container was moved nearby them on a dolly. Kylie didn't ask, but she was sure it was the body of the man upstairs. Curtis pulled her tighter into his arms. She would be glad when this thing was over.

They worked for another three hours. Then they broke for lunch. The security team, all of them armed, showed up about ten minutes before they left. They seemed to be ready for just about anything. And as they walked out of the place, Kylie couldn't help but look back at the stairs.

"Soon. Soon this will be all over, and things will be normal again."

Kylie looked at Mrs. Hunter.

"Well, as normal as it can be, I suppose."

"Curtis thinks he'll come the day before we're supposed to go and find it. What do you think?"

Annamarie, as she insisted on being called, shrugged.

"Do you think he'll give up once he sees the fence and the guards?"

"Oh, no, dear. He'll think of this as a challenge for him. Men like him think that they're invincible. They have so much given to them because of fear that they actually believe that they'll get whatever they want simply because."

Kylie started to ask what when she realized she knew. "It's like when I was a child. I never had to want anything. I simply had it. Daddy didn't have to give me everything, but he did. Because he loved me."

"That's true, but in this case, the case of the LaMancusas, I think it was more of a getting it because someone might have told him no. Or because he wanted it because someone else had it. Not that he wanted or needed it, just that he didn't have it. He doesn't seem to be a terribly stable man."

Kylie had to agree. The way things were going, she doubted that any of them were all that stable. When they pulled up in front of the restaurant, she was happy to see her dad. He was being pushed in his wheelchair by a very pretty nurse who she'd met that morning.

By the time they were settled around the big table and lunch was ordered, she sat back in her chair. People were shouting over one another. Laughter was prevalent. There were some low said bad words, but Annamarie must have had great hearing because she would glare at the offender when they were said. Noisy and nosy people talked around and to each other, and she was going to be a part of this family. And she'd never been happier in her life.

Chapter 14

Mary closed the phone with a snap. She was getting angry, and when she was angry, blood was shed. She looked at her watch and wondered where the hell her brother was. He should have checked in over an hour ago. She looked over at her grandson and wondered how the hell she'd stood him for all these years.

"Did he get it?"

She shook her head at this question.

"Mother fuck. Now, what do we do? Wait for them to call us up and say, 'did you lose something? Well, we found it.' Not likely."

"He still has time to call us. They might not know exactly where the money is in the place. For all we know, they could be tearing out each wall to try and find it." She didn't really think so, but he didn't have to know that. One thing about her brother Billy, he was prompt.

Eric snorted. Mary walked to the desk and started to pull the little book toward her. She decided that it was time to see if he knew as much as she hoped he did. The man had to be smarter than she'd been seeing since she'd taken over his care when his mother had left.

"There used to be a combination to that safe. I don't suppose, when you were looking around here, you found it?" She opened the book, and the handwriting of her late husband jumped out at her. "Your grandda had the worst handwriting."

"No. I looked at everything." He flopped down in the chair and glared. Mary ignored him. "I tried to get it out of dear old dad, but he wasn't talking. The 'M' in the book? Do you think she might know?"

She'd been taken care of, she'd told him. "It was your mother if you really want to know. I'm not sure why we didn't simply kill her off too, but something happened."

"What did you do?" He leaned forward in the chair as if she was telling him a bedtime story. "Did you have her killed, or did you hire someone? I never knew her, and whenever I brought her up, Dad would knock the shit out of me. I kind of figured that something happened between them."

There was some falling out, but Mary couldn't remember. She was pretty sure it had something to do with her parents, Michelle's. Mary knew that they loved the fact that Eric, Vaughn back then, was going to be their first grandson. There was the older daughter, one from a previous marriage, that Michelle had had, but not a grandson. The younger girl… Mary couldn't remember her name, was too young to sell off, but they'd been waiting on that. Mary had thought they could have used the older girl, but she disappeared right after Michelle had been locked up.

"Your mother was a whore. And she'd have sold off the family if the price had been right." Mary continued looking through the book. Most of it was nothing she could figure out because her husband hadn't been very forthcoming in what he had been up to until he needed her to fix things while he'd been in prison.

She also thought of her daughter-in-law. Michelle hadn't been bad at all. In fact, she was good to the family. And when she'd find any information out, she'd slip it to her father-in-law when he'd been in one of many stays or call him up. Mary thought that was what had pissed her off.

That's when she'd bullied Vaughn into thinking that his lovely little wife was going to the Feds. She was, but only when they made her. But as far as Mary knew, Michelle had never said a word. At least not until after Vaughn had tied her to a chair and kept her doped up, then hooked her on the harder shit. Then she'd been too unstable for anyone to control. She'd tried several times to kill her husband and Mary. When she'd gone after her, Mary had put the fear of no money into her son. That had worked.

"We should find your mother. I bet she knows more than she let on." She knew a great deal, and Mary knew it. "I know where she's staying. How about you and I make a little trip and collect her?"

Eric was already nodding. "We could do that. I would love to see the look on her face when she sees how much I've taken over the family business."

Mary didn't comment but stood too. If they left now, they could be there before she killed the little cocksucker. Run the business? Out of business was more like it. She knew he was in deep to the sharks. And there were days, like today, that she wished they'd come and try to collect.

It took them over two hours to get to the little town. And another forty minutes to find the little place she'd been staying. Or at least where the card had said she'd been staying. They drove up and down the same street four times before they went to a convenience store and asked.

"The Jefferson place, you say?"

Eric nodded and smiled. Mary thought he looked insane but didn't comment.

"Jefferson. There used to be a Madison family that lived on that street. Might have been about thirty years ago now. Nice family them. We had Christmas dinner at their house. His missus could really make a turkey moist. I used to ask my own missus—"

"The Jeffersons. Do you know the Jeffersons?" Mary was getting a headache listening to the man go on about a turkey. "I'm sorry. I just need to find them. They've been so nice to my daughter-in-law."

The man seemed to be thinking over whether or not he wanted to be helpful. Mary couldn't really blame him. She'd nearly pulled out her gun just then, and that wouldn't help anyone.

"So's far as I know, there ain't been a Jefferson on that street in forever. If you want, you can have the phonebook, not that many people use phones nowadays. Not with all those cell towers—" He seemed to realize that getting off subject might get him yelled at again. Or killed, Mary thought. "Here you go. Have at it."

The phonebook wasn't all that thick, and there wasn't a Jefferson in the entire thing. There wasn't even a Jefferson Street or any other kind of street, avenue, or road on the little map provided in the front. They thanked the man and walked out of the store. Eric had a twenty-four pack of beer and some snacks for the ride home.

Something was off. For nearly twenty some years, she'd gotten a card from the Jeffersons on Davidson Avenue. Now come to find out, there wasn't even a house with that number on it. Mary got into the car and looked into the store. The clerk was missing.

"Mother fucknuts. I think we've been made." She started to get out of the car and take care of the problem she was sure was brewing when a cruiser pulled in beside them. Mary put the car into reverse and backed out of the space. She figured that if the clerk had called the cops, she had about a minute to get out of there.

"What is it?" Eric opened his door, but she was on the move now. "What the fuck are you doing? Trying to kill my ass? We've been made how?"

"I think your mommy dear's caretakers are about as real as the house. As in it's all made up, and she really is with the Feds." Mary turned down the first street she came to and turned off the lights. She thought a cruiser drove by, but couldn't be sure. "We have to ditch this car and get something else. Are you good a hotwiring one?"

He looked at her blankly, and she swore again. He was about as useless as tits on a boar hog. "Why?" was all he could say? Shit. She was going to kill him tonight, leave him in this car, and walk away from it all.

But she knew that she couldn't. Not only was there the money, and that was a big, expensive reason, but now she knew that Michelle wasn't as goody-two-shoes as she'd led her husband to believe she was. Vaughn senior had thought she could do no wrong.

The car proved to be easy to steal. She walked around the parking lot at the mall for eight minutes before someone left their car running and went inside. It wouldn't be long before it was reported, but it would get them to another car that was less noticeable. The local impound lot was where she wanted them to go. The baby screaming in the back seat nearly had her shoot it, but she took out the car seat and left it on the sidewalk. She didn't want kidnapping added to the theft charges. Laughing, she got into the minivan and pulled away.

"I don't know what the hell you think is so funny. We damned near got caught back there. And all because you wanted to find my mom."

Mary couldn't help it; she doubled up her fist and hit him. He might have been all right had his head not snapped against the window across from him. She reached for and found his pulse and was disappointed she couldn't roll his ass out while she was speeding down the highway.

She was tempted but didn't do it. Mary could think of a few reasons for keeping him. One of them being a human shield for her if the Feds caught up with them. Laughing again, she drove back home. The impound lot hadn't had a lot of choices, but she did take the one with the most dust on it. Lucky for her, it had a full tank of gas too.

~~~

"Charlie said that they left the place over twenty minutes ago. The guy they had there tried to stall them until the police arrived, but the woman was getting antsy."

Curtis watched his brother stretch out on the couch in his office.

"What do you want to do now?"

"I want to go home and make love to Kylie." Curtis flushed. He hadn't meant to say that out loud.

Royce laughed. "Sounds like a plan. I might go home and do the same." Royce stood when Curtis did. "Can I ask you something?"

Curtis was immediately nervous. The last time he'd been asked that, he had been suckered into a job he didn't want to do. He looked cautiously at his brother. "Shoot, but know I have the right to refuse to answer."

Royce nodded. "What would you have done if Daniel had told you he was in love with Kylie?"

Curtis was shocked by the question. Not so much the question, but that he'd been thinking the same thing just today.

"Would you have given her up to him?"

"No." He shook his head as he put on his jacket. "No. I thought at first that I could, but I just realized that I wouldn't have been able to. I have loved her for so long that…no, that's not right. I've loved her for my entire life, and I couldn't have given her up no matter how much Daniel had told me he loved her. Lucky for me, he didn't."

Royce nodded. "Figured as much. I've been thinking the same thing about Kasey. What would have happened to us had she not stopped me to badge in? What would my life have been like without her or little Lee in it?"

What? Curtis thought. *Nothing.* He knew that as surely as he was standing there. And he was pretty sure that Royce thought the same thing. They both rode the elevator down in silence. Jay York was waiting for them with a smile.

"The car is out front, sir, as is Miss Washington. She's none too happy with you for making her sit out there with no information." Jay smiled. "I hope you don't mind, but I had a dozen roses put in there for you. My niece loves when Royce does that for her."

"I wondered where those were coming from." Royce patted Jay on the back. "I owe you big time. How about a night on the town with those cronies of yours? We can…"

Curtis left the building and climbed into the waiting limo. He didn't stop moving across the seat until he had Kylie pressed against the back of it and her mouth moving under his. He'd missed her.

The kiss ended when he was pulled from her by a ringing phone. He picked up the car phone and answered the driver. They were going house hunting, and the first house was close at hand.

"You said we'd look after we were married. We have plenty of time for looking. We have someplace to live now."

He grinned as he sat her on his lap.

"Do you think you can behave for ten minutes?"

"Nope. And we need a house soon. I want to get anything we want to be changed done before we start on the building downtown. Did you ever think of a name?"

"Yes. But don't change the subject. Where are we going? I thought the house on my father's street was going to be fine."

He winked as the door to the limo was opened.

"Curtis, what have you done?"

He'd done a great deal today. First of all, this house. There were four more on the itinerary, but this was the one he wanted for her. He handed her out of the car and watched her face to see how she liked it. He was thrilled when she tried to speak several times before she looked at him.

"You can afford this?"

He nodded, not even insulted that she had to ask.

"But Curtis, this thing is huge. How on earth are we going to keep it clean?"

He threw back his head and laughed. "We can. Trust me. Come on. Let's go have a look. I'm pretty sure you're going to love it too."

The double oak door had sold him. He loved the etched glass almost as much as he had the big entranceway. He opened the doors for her and let her walk in alone. It was the only way to see this place. He'd made a deal with the realtor, telling her he'd pay the asking price if she let him show Kylie the house himself.

The parquet floors were polished to a high sheen. He let her walk around the large opening and then pointed to the massive chandelier in the center of the room. There were three open doorways that lead off the opening, and if she stood in the middle of the one across from the door, she'd be able to see the large winding staircase.

To the left of where they were standing was the living room. A fireplace big enough to roast an ox sat along the far wall. Windows and doors lined the entire wall, and the doors opened onto a large lawn that had a pool as well as a pool house. He couldn't wait to see it in the spring with her. The other door led to the dining room.

This is where he wanted to see her. Entertaining guests that the firm would placate would be her specialty. Curtis thought of the massive table he could see there with a dozen chairs down each side. Oak and walnut china cabinets graced either side of the room and more windows and doors, all glass, let sunlight, or in this case, evening light filter in. Another large chandelier graced the middle of the room and would be perfectly centered over the table. She turned to him and smiled.

"You did this on purpose, didn't you?"

He tried to pretend that he had no idea what she was talking about, but she looked so cute standing there.

"You knew if I saw this house first, then nothing else would do. What would you have done if I didn't like this one?"

He walked toward her, smiling. "I knew you would. Do you want to see the rest, or are you happy with this one?"

He pulled her into his arms and then to his mouth. He loved kissing her and wanted to do so much more. He pressed her against the wall when she pulled back. He looked down at her face and realized just how much he loved her.

"I have something important to tell you."

He licked along her throat and grinned when she stuttered.

"Curtis, please, it's important."

"So is this." He continued down her skin until she jerked his head up and glared at him. "Okay, tell me so that I can get back to work here."

"The name of the safe house. I know what it is." She held him tighter when he tried to pull away. "Royce James Hunter House. After your dad."

He stopped moving and looked at her. "My dad? I thought you'd name it after your dad. Why…I don't understand." His dad had been a great man. A wonderful father and a well-loved man to those who knew him. But to name a building after him? Curtis thought of what that would mean to his mom. "Does Mom know?"

Kylie nodded then shook her head.

"Which, baby? She either does, or she doesn't."

"I asked her his name and how he had died. She told me it was saving a kid. Did you know that the city wanted to name a street after him?"

He had, but after some quick talking from his mom, they had decided not to. What would she say now? To this? "We'll have to okay it from Mom. She wasn't all that thrilled back then. I'm not sure how she'll take this."

Kylie smiled and put her hand on his cheek. "She'll love it. She told me that she wished now she'd of let them do it. She was too raw back then and was also worried about you. She said she thought you took it the hardest of all her children because you and your dad were so close."

They had been, too. He held her as he thought of their times together, their time when it was just the two of them, and he missed it. Curtis thought that calling the center after his dad was fine. It was time. He pulled away just a little, and she looked up at him. "I love you." Kylie smiled. "I love you so very much. And I think that this is a spectacular idea."

She put her head back onto his chest, and he could feel her laughter. "Of course, it is. I'm good at wonderful, spectacular ideas."

Curtis showed her the rest of the house. He could tell that she loved it as much as he had. The rooms needed to be updated, and the carpet replaced, but the overall structure of the house was perfect.

"We'll have Stone Construction come in and do the kitchen. It needs some cabinets moved, as well as some of the bigger appliances that I want to have put in need more space. Then you can call in someone to decorate, or you can. Either way, we should be able to move in, in about a month. Sound good?"

She nodded and walked around what would become their bedroom. She was twirling around the room when his phone rang. As he answered, he was smiling, and, as soon as he heard the voice at the other end, he turned his back to her. He didn't want to ruin this for her. But she knew and came to his side as Vaughn LaMancusa made his demands. The bastard knew that his mom was in the Federal Witness Program.

Chapter 15

Vaughn, what he was calling himself now, sat at his desk and glared at his grandmother. His head still ached from hitting the window, and she had yet to apologize to him. He had a feeling she thought he owed her one, but he just couldn't do it. She'd hit him, for Christ's sake.

"Where the hell would they have taken her?" She'd asked this question three times now, and he didn't bother answering. She didn't want an answer anyway, so he didn't even try. "I mean, that was simply dirty pool on their part to send me cards every year with updates of her progress."

Vaughn actually thought it was brilliant, but didn't say that again. He was beginning to think his grandmother had a mean streak in her. He watched her pace the room and wondered aloud if she'd heard from her brother.

"No. I'm pretty sure he's either dead, or he's run off with my money. I'll hunt him down and cut his balls off if he—"

"Your money?"

She looked back at him with confusion.

"You said if he ran off with your money. I'm pretty sure that it would be more mine than yours. My father is the one who would have left it to me. Your husband was dead in prison. Mine at least would have—"

"It was a simple slip of the tongue. Don't read too much into it." She continued to pace, but he watched her closely now. "As I was saying, I don't think he's run off, but with him, it's hard to tell. I have been trying to reach his cell since yesterday and nothing. He's more than likely dead. What did that prick say when you told him that he would either give us the building or the contents? You didn't sound too thrilled about his answer."

"He said that he would take it under consideration. As if I didn't mean shit to him. I actually heard him laugh at me. I can't stand when people don't take me seriously. I'm going to have to do something that makes him sit up and take notice of me. So we need another plan." He took out a sheet of paper, and because he knew it would irritate her, he ripped it in half but way off center. She was a nut about things being dead on. "We need to find out if the money was found. I'm thinking it wasn't because the paper or the news would have had something on about it." He started to write this on one half of the paper only to have her jerk it from him and hand him another sheet. This one nearly perfect in size and shape. Lowering his head so she wouldn't see, he had to fight hard not to laugh. She was way too easy.

"I agree. And don't let that go to your head." She sat down in the chair across from him. "So the thing we have to figure out is if they didn't find the money, then either it's not there, or they simply didn't look in the right place."

Well, duh, he thought. "Okay. So we need to sneak inside, figure out where they have looked, and try to see if we can do a better job of it."

"Sure. And have you been paying attention to anything

I've said to you tonight?" Her tone said that she knew he hadn't. His gun slipped out of his pocket and into his lap. He was going to end up killing her, he knew it. "There are about ten armed guards around the place. Not to mention dogs. I fucking hate dogs. And then there are the security lights. I wonder if they have stock in the electric company for as much as they have to be spending just to keep the bad guys away."

Apparently, he should have paid attention. Guards, guns, and dogs were not what he'd expected. Though he should have. They were aware as much as he was what might be inside the building. And he now knew that the Hunters had more money than most celebrities. Vaughn put money in the column and circled it. They really needed to…

"Mother fuck, what day is this?"

Mary grinned when she looked up.

"Mother fuck. I forgot the money I owe. I have to get it over to them right fucking now."

He stood up just as the office door opened. Three men dressed in black, even black sunglasses in the middle of the night, muscled their way in. He was held to his chair with a nine millimeter to his head, as was Mary. Neither of them moved. Then his worst nightmare walked in.

"Nice place you have here, Vaughny. Might have to purchase it from you when this deal is done." He sat in the chair next to Mary and looked at her. "You, I know. And I'm pretty sure you remember me as well."

She nodded. That surprised him. Then he remembered that someone had been feeding him information. But she didn't look to be very friendly with him. Fear was in her eyes. She glanced over at him and then back at the man.

"You're McKnight, Lambert McKnight." He nodded, and she looked at him again. "He's a mob boss out of Italy."

He seemed so pleased with her answer, but for some reason, it didn't lessen the fact that he was one scary person. He leaned back in the chair and looked at him. His smile in no way comforted Vaughn.

"You disappoint me, Vaughny. I expected you to come to the docks like a good boy, and you didn't show. And now today you didn't call me to tell me that you have some money stashed somewhere." He tisked and shook his head. "I'm very unhappy. Do you know what happens when I'm unhappy?"

Before Vaughn could shake his head no, McKnight pulled a gun out of his coat and shot his grandmother in the head. She fell over backward as the chair hit the floor. Vaughn started screaming and only shut up when McKnight stood up and pointed the gun at him.

"Please don't kill me." He was whining, but he was breathing. "Please. I'll give you anything you want if you don't kill me."

"Oh, you're going to do that anyway, but I find that I need you now." McKnight sat back down. "Now, here's the plan, Vaughny boy. You're going to tell me everything you know about that money and the people who are thinking to take what belongs to me."

With shaky hands, he reached for the file he had with the clippings in it. One of his thugs picked up Mary and tossed her over his shoulder. He started cussing when blood dripped onto his shirt. McKnight assured him that Vaughny would be more than happy to pay for the dry cleaning. He found himself nodding before he could think how the hell that would work if they killed him. And he was positive he was as good as dead.

The clippings, he read. Thoroughly. Then he read the notebook. He didn't know why he thought that so funny, but

Vaughn sat quietly and tried not to bring attention to himself. After an hour, the door behind him opened again, and one of the thugs McKnight brought with him walked in carrying a tray of food. Vaughn stood up and started for the table. He was starving.

"If you want something to eat, then I would suggest that you make yourself something. This is mine."

Vaughn flushed at McKnight's words. As Vaughn started to the door, McKnight spoke again.

"And if you leave this house without my permission, I will hunt you down and cut your throat only to stand over you and watch you bleed to death."

Vaughn turned slowly and looked at the man now sitting at his little table. His voice had been so calm, so easy going, that it would have sounded like a joke. Might have sounded like a joke but for the large gun sitting in his one hand and the fork with food on it in the other. The man wasn't just scary but terrifying. Vaughn walked to the kitchen on jellylike legs, suddenly not very hungry any longer.

~~~

Royce watched his brother. Curtis wasn't a man who got ruffled, nor did he get thrown off. But he was both. If the circumstances were a little different, he'd laugh at him. But right now, everything was riding on their next steps. No one wanted anyone to get hurt.

"What do you suppose that guy, Trust, what was his angle in this whole thing?"

Royce reached for the thick file on his desk and opened it. He didn't point out to his brother that he'd asked that same question not ten minutes ago but answered him again. "According to his file at work, nothing. But Mann had been monitoring his actions for a few years, and since the transfer of the building owner changed, he'd been a tad more active. Mann thinks that he is either in with one of the families or simply one of those people who came in and took the goods when the work was all done." Royce thought it was more than that, but didn't comment. He had a feeling that he was related to LaMancusa somehow.

"So he knew that we were going to try and see about the money. How? Who might have told him? Mann?"

Royce nodded.

"So who do you think he told? LaMancusa?"

"More than likely. You got the phone call yesterday, so we can assume that he knows more than he did. And the fact that he knows his mother is alive and kicking means someone besides the Feds knew. It was more than likely the older woman that was with him when he went searching for her." The phone ringing made him glare, but he answered it. He'd told his secretary to hold his calls.

"I just found out that Trust is actually William "Billy" Salinas. He's a half-uncle to our little buddy Vaughn. And his half-sister is none other than Mary Salinas LaMancusa, wife of Vaughn Senior."

Royce felt the hair on his arms rise.

"Mary and Billy, as he likes to be called, were united by family when her mother married his dad. Salinas adopted Mary after a couple of years married to her mother, and the rest, as they say, was history."

Royce told his brother and put the phone on speaker so they both could listen as Mann continued. "There was another sibling, but she was brutally raped just after the marriage, and she killed herself. Rumor had it that it was Billy, but as no one pressed the matter, it was forgotten. Mary ended up marrying senior when she was seventeen while Billy was in prison for something else."

"So did he join the family too?" Curtis started making a flow chart of sorts, and Royce watched him. It looked like a family tree. "If he did, then that explains how he knew."

"It doesn't look like it. And if he had, it wasn't on the up and up. His crimes got progressively worse as the years went by until he was put away about eighteen years ago on a drug charge. Three times he was out." They heard papers shuffle around. "The reason we never knew about him being related, I suppose, is because he never did anything similar to the family. Bank robberies and murder while Billy sold drugs and dealt in prostitution as well as arms."

"Then how the hell did he end up in the Feds?" Royce didn't want to think about how the man had accomplished to get there. Money? Blackmail? "I mean, you said he had worked there for nine years."

"Yes, William Trust did work for us. Out in California. It wasn't until recently that we figured out this man was not the man who worked for us. Someone came across the real Trust's body about two years ago. For reasons I can't go into, we never confronted the man we killed yesterday, but suffice it to say, he was being watched very closely."

They knew. Or someone did. Someone in the operation knew that Trust was part of the family and kept him close to see if they could get information from him. Curtis looked as if he had figured it out as well. And he wasn't happy about it.

"So instead of taking care of the problem, you left it so that someone had to get shot years later. What if my future wife or one of the other men and women there had gotten shot instead? Would you have come clean with this and admitted your mistake?" The door opening behind him and their mother stepping into the room didn't slow Curtis. He was pissed. "You mother fucking ass hole, the next time I see you, I'm going to kick your fucking ass and then break every bone in your body."

"Curtis."

He turned to the sound of his name and saw not only Mom but Kylie as well. Royce waited for his mom to yell at him, but Kylie continued to speak.

"You can't blame this man for someone else's mistakes."

"The fuck I can't." Curtis flushed when Royce cleared his throat. "Sorry. But you could have been hurt. I want...no, I need you. I can't stop...you could have been killed."

"Yes. And you could have been too. But neither of us was, and the only one that died is the bad guy. We won this time. Let's make it a trend and not bite the hand of the messenger."

Curtis walked toward her, and their mom moved out of the way. Royce was pretty sure that neither of them remembered that they were in the room with them either when they finally came together. Royce felt his own face heat when his mom cleared her throat.

"I love you." Curtis said after a few seconds of simply holding Kylie. "I'm so sorry. I should have...but every time I think about what could have been? I get pissed."

"I have more information for you if you want it. Or I can call back later. I have nothing more to do today than listen to a big overgrown baby get his ass kicked by his fiancée." Royce laughed as Mann and Curtis said something low. Kylie slapped him on the shoulder as they both made their way to the desk again.

"What do you have? And so you know, I'm not sure I'm any less pi...mad at you. I reserve the right to still wipe the floor up with you." Mann laughed before continuing with his information.

They had known about Mary and her working in the household. But until they'd spoken to Michelle, they hadn't known that she was related to LaMancusa. The pieces were finally tumbling together. The woman known as Mary Phyllis was the head of the LaMancusa family.

Then there was the information that they'd found at the home of Billy. He'd been very well informed. And the building on Biloxi had been his biggest concern. The man had blueprints from back when the building had been built, as well as the plans that Curtis had recently had finished up on the renovations to the building.

"The architect, Peter Jacobson, is dead. His house was ransacked a few days ago, and his body found in his car in the trunk. Didn't put the two together until today. Seems that the man had a major gambling problem as well as a few secrets he was keeping from his partner. The lover sort, not business. Jacobson had a girlfriend, boyfriend, as well as a wife. The man was way in over his head. We thought that one of them or all of them did it. The man had AIDS and spread it to all of them."

"Oh my."

Royce looked at his mom.

"To be so careless with other people's lives. I do hope you have no plans of using that firm again."

Royce nodded, and Mann continued. "Careless wasn't the half of it, but nothing to do with what we found. Billy also had a hell of an arsenal. And I mean heavy stuff. I'm pretty sure his next plans were to blow up the building after he found what he wanted. There was enough dynamite in the place to take out an entire city block."

"So, he knew about the robbery and what might have been in our building almost before you did." Curtis picked up

Kylie and put her on his lap as he spoke. Royce did the same with his wife when he needed assurance. He was pretty sure his brother didn't even realize that he'd done it.

"Pretty much. We have an address for LaMancusa. It was difficult because the house hasn't changed hands in nearly forty years. It belonged to one of the wives of the original LaMancusa. No one ever laid claim to it after she passed, and its taxes had been paid when due. There was no reason to believe it wasn't being sold off or willed down."

He gave them the address with the understanding that they were to not go near it. "We have men watching the building now. It's only a matter of time before we move in and take him. It's now within the Feds' hands."

Both Kylie and Curtis snorted. Royce agreed with them. So far, his family had done more to solve this case in a few short weeks than any of them had done in all the time after the robbery. Royce didn't doubt that they were better equipped than they had been at first, but he still didn't trust them to keep his family safe.

After the phone call, Royce called his other brothers. It was time they stepped up their own security here at work and at their homes. They met for dinner at his mom's house, and Kasey was going to meet them there as well. He needed his wife and son to be near him and couldn't wait to see them both again. He loved his wife very, very much.

Chapter 16

The drive to the house was quiet. Curtis tried his best not to think about how much they had learned in the past ten or so hours, but his mind was awhirl of it. He glanced over at Kylie and knew that she was thinking too hard. He decided that they needed to relax, and he knew just how to make that happen. He pulled off the road onto a service road he knew hadn't been used in a decade.

"What is it? Are we having car trouble?"

He heard the panic in her voice, but before he could tell her anything, she was out of the car. Cursing, he got out to follow her. "There isn't anything wrong. Not with the car anyway." She stopped, trying to get the hood open and stared at him. "I have a major problem and need you to help me with it."

She looked confused for all of two seconds and then leaned against the car. "What sort of problem? Is it something that I might be able to help you with, or something I *can* help you with? Or do we need to call in the professionals?"

"I'm pretty sure you can fix it. Come here, and I'll show you what I need."

She shook her head.

"Kylie, come here, please. I want to bend you over this car and fuck you until neither of us can move."

Again, she shook her head. "I'd rather suck your cock until you come down my throat. Take you deep into my mouth and cup your balls until you can't hold back."

Curtis had to lean against the door. Suddenly, his knees were weak with need. He started to undo his belt when she moved toward him, taking off her blouse. It wasn't until she was standing before him with only her skirt on that he realized he'd forgotten what he'd been doing. When she dropped before him and finished his task, he spoke.

"You're going to pay for messing up my plans." He watched her remove his belt and unsnap his pants. As she moved his pants to his knees, he felt his eyes roll to the back of his head. "Kylie, please, honey, let me fuck you before it's too late."

Her soft laughter was sexy. His cock seemed to leap toward her mouth, and she obliged it. Licking along his length, he moaned deep in his throat. Christ, she was going to have him begging before she even got started.

Her mouth was warm and wet. He gripped the handle on the car door with one hand while he held himself as still as he could. When she took him into her mouth and then to the back of her throat Curtis rocked his hips forward and deepened her kiss of him.

Every time he thought he was going to come, she'd change positions. His balls ached for release, and his body glistened with sweat. Wrapping his hand into her hair, he tried to guide her to finish him, but she stopped. No amount of pressure could make her do what his entire body needed.

"I'm going to finish myself if you don't give me my release. I swear to you that I'm going to come so hard when I do that you'll never swallow all of me." He rocked again and hoped she'd help him. But all she did was lean back on her heels and look up at him. He was nearly to the point of begging.

"I want to feel you come all over me. Will you do that for me?"

He nodded because speech at this point would have been impossible. When she stood up, he reached for her, and she backed away.

"Not yet. I want to be ready for you."

In seconds, she was naked. He watched her move to the hood of the car and lay across it. Her legs were open to the moonlight and to his view. Christ, there would never be a sexier pose that would take his breath away like this one was. Moving to stand between her open legs, he watched her slide her fingers deep into her soaking pussy.

"You're so beautiful."

She cupped her breast and tweaked at her nipple while he gripped his cock in his fist.

"I'm going to fuck you. Coming over, you will not be enough."

"Please, Curtis. I need to come too. Sucking on you, feeling your cock touch the back of my throat was amazing."

He touched her pussy with the head of his cock and felt her suck at him. She was as needy as he was. His body seemed to have all the time it needed to make this last. Moving slowly in and out of her, he watched her rise up off the hood every time he pulled out. Resting his hands on her upright knees, he held her while he took her.

She was his. And he was hers. Never in his life would anyone ever mean as much to him as this woman did. He leaned down over her and took her mouth. She tasted of him and sex. He growled against her.

Curtis lifted her up, and she wrapped around him. Pressing her against the door, he buried into her as deeply as he could. She held onto his shoulders as if he were her lifeline, and he knew in that moment that she was his.

"I want a child with you. As soon as we can, I want to see you swollen with our child." He moved back and slammed into her again. "Tell me, Kylie, tell me you want it too."

Her release was amazing. She screamed out her answer even as her body milked him. His cock, already primed for release, seemed to lengthen and expand as his balls seemingly exploded outward. Pounding into her body, he felt his cock touch her deep, bury his seed into her. Curtis saw stars as he came. His vision blurred as he rocked into her.

When he could move, he realized two things at once. His pants were tangled around his legs and that his phone was ringing. Careful not to drop the woman in his arms, he worked his jeans down and off his legs so he could set her down and ignored the phone. He was setting her in the passenger seat as he heard the chime that he had a voice message.

"You do know that we could have been caught here, right?"

He grinned at her question as he handed her the pants she'd had on.

"Not to mention that, had we been caught, your mother would have murdered us both."

"Probably. But then again, we'd have this memory of why she was pissed at us and not really give a shit." She grinned back as she pulled her shirt over her head, not bothering with her bra. He loved the way her breasts bounced unfettered the way they were.

"True."

He pulled on his pants as she watched him. He could see

that she wanted to say something, and he let her have her own way about it.

"Curtis, were you serious?"

He turned to look at her as he tossed his belt in the back of the car. He wasn't going to bother when they were so close to home. He leaned over the hood of the car where she sat and looked down at her.

"I'm rarely not serious. But what do you mean?" He wanted to take her into his arms again but knew that she would be sore. He hadn't exactly been gentle with her.

"Do you really want a baby with me? I mean now, do you really want to have a baby with me?"

He pulled her out then. And when she tried to look away from him, he held her face in both his hands. He looked deeply into her eyes as he answered her. "I love you with all my heart, and having a child with you would make me that happiest man on earth." He kissed her softly but lovingly. "But only if that's what you want too. I would never want you to do something that you—"

She put her hand over his mouth. "I love you too. And I want your child so badly that I can't think beyond it happening. I do love you more than anything in this world."

He held her until she shivered. He'd forgotten about the cold night and helped her into the car. Walking to his side, he smiled. Things were going to be better now. They had their entire lives to be together, and he knew that while it would never be enough, he was going to make it his life's mission to make her never regret falling in love with him. Picking up his phone, he listened to the message and smiled. It seemed that LaMancusa wanted to meet to work out a deal.

~~~

"I left him a message. He'll have to...he'll call back. He'll have to." Vaughn looked at the man at his desk and cringed when he lifted his gun and pointed at him. "I can't make him answer his phone."

"No, but had you not fucked this up in the first place, we'd all be a lot better off. You have to be the most incompetent person I've ever met. How the hell did you spring from your father's loins?"

Vaughn wanted to point out that he had gotten this far, but thought it would be a mistake. Knew it would be, actually. McKnight was not a stable man. Vaughn glanced over at the dead man lying next to his chair. All he'd done to end up there was to ask if Vaughn had wanted any coffee when he'd been going to get his boss some. Apparently, he wasn't to speak to him and had paid dearly for the mistake.

"You want to join him?"

Vaughn looked back at McKnight.

"I could arrange it if you'd like. I'm pretty sure you've given me all that you can, and I don't really need another partner right now."

"Hunter is going to meet me. He's expecting me." Stupid reason, he knew, but it was all he had to hopefully live another day. "He's not stupid. I'm pretty sure he wouldn't come to meet me if he saw you there too."

The gun was put back on the desk, and while Vaughn was relieved, he didn't relax. He was reasonably sure that he wanted to keep him on his toes. He glanced down at his watch again. Five hours before he had to meet the man responsible for fucking up his life. Well, not all of it. He'd not been the one who'd gotten him into this mess, but merely the one who had made it worse.

He tried to remember the details that he'd given Hunter. It should have been simple, but since he hadn't written them down, he kept forgetting some of them. He knew that he was to meet him at the mall, but...

"Do you know how long it takes to get over to where he said he'd meet you?" McKnight startled him out of his thoughts. "Hello, I asked you, do you know how long it takes to get to the mall? Are you that stupid?"

"Forty minutes. It was built on that end of town after my father passed away." He snapped his mouth closed, realizing he was babbling. "Forty minutes."

"We'll leave here in an hour. I want to get into a good position to see the man who outsmarted you." His laughter made Vaughn's skin crawl. "Of course, I'm pretty sure that the next door neighbor's dog could do that, but I might be able to persuade him to enter into a contract with me. I could use a man who has come up from nothing and become the man that he supposedly is."

He'd been sitting at his computer when Vaughn had come back up from the kitchen. McKnight had not only figured out which Hunter owned the building but had a complete rundown on the man as well as his family. And knowing the fact that he was now engaged to the daughter of the man Vaughn had beaten up. Kylie Washington and Curtis Hunter were set to marry in five weeks.

"He doesn't strike me as the joining type. I mean, he seems so straight about everything." Vaughn hadn't realized he'd spoken out loud until McKnight turned to him again. "I'm sorry."

McKnight shrugged. "If he doesn't join forces with me, then he'll be as dead as that man." He looked over at the man in question. "I'm easy. Yes or no. Either way, I'm a happy man."

Insane was more like it. Vaughn licked his lips when

McKnight took another line of his stuff. Vaughn was shaking with need now, and he wanted to knock the other man away and bury his nose in the stuff. It had been hours since he'd had a good hit, and he was hurting badly. He was about to ask for it when the door opened behind them. He nearly wet himself.

"Car's ready. Guns are loaded too." This man looked twice the size as the one on the floor. When the man looked at the one near Vaughn, he nodded toward him. "Want I should put him with the others?"

McKnight nodded. Others? There had been his grandmother and this one. Had he killed his staff as well? He wanted to ask but was afraid of what his answer would be. *"Yes,"* maybe, and, *"you're going to join them."*

Vaughn felt his bladder loosen. He stood suddenly and didn't even stop when the gun was lifted again. He dashed past the man in the doorway and down the hall. The laughter that followed him didn't faze him as much as not wetting his pants did. He made it to the toilet just as another spasm hit him. Christ, he was going to piss himself.

It took him nearly twenty minutes before he moved out into the hall. He'd had a good talking with himself and felt marginally better about things. Not perfect, but better. He walked into his office to see McKnight standing next to the safe in his office.

"You know the combination to this sucker?" He spun the dial again and looked back at him. "It more than likely has more money in it than what's in the wall."

"I tried. Even as I beat my father to death, I couldn't get him to tell it to me. I think it's in that book, but I can't figure out how." He sat down again but didn't reach for it. The book held all sorts of secrets, he was sure. "Mary didn't know it either. We think it has something to do with my mother, but she's gone into hiding by the Feds."

"Yeah, I know. We tried to find her thinking to get to control you with her. But it wasn't until afterward that we figured out you didn't know shit about her either. Mary did, but she wasn't giving her up. I think she figured your mother was useless to her." He laughed. "I guess we were both wrong about her."

He thought he was talking about Mary and him, but didn't comment. Vaughn didn't know she had existed until a few days ago. How could he have known whether or not she knew dick?

The phone rang. He reached for it, as McKnight did. When he backed up with that smile on his face that said, *"go ahead, you won't be around all that long anyway,"* Vaughn picked up the phone with a shaky hand.

"Hello, we were calling to speak to the owners of the household. We were wondering if you had a few minutes to answer some questions. We're asking all your neighbors who they would vote for this fall."

Vaughn glanced up at McKnight, sure he was laughing at him. "I don't vote." He nearly hung up the phone when he heard the voice on the other end, speak again. This time, the hair on his arms danced, and his blood ran cold.

"No, but you should have. Then you would have been in fucking jail instead of screwing around in my life. There's been a change of plans."

Vaughn sat down hard when Hunter spoke again, this time quicker than before.

"You'll meet me at the building in one hour. If you don't, then I'm taking the money out, and you'll never see a thin dime of it."

The phone went dead. He laid the receiver into the cradle and closed his eyes. This wasn't going to make McKnight happy and would probably get him killed. He turned to the man when he thought he could do so without begging for his life. "That was Hunter. He said I either meet him at the newspaper in one hour or he'd take the money now."

McKnight shook his head, then smiled.

"He doesn't sound as if he is worried about us."

"He's not because he doesn't know about me. That's because you've been a pussy about this for so long he knows you'll be begging him to take the money so you won't go to prison. But he doesn't know not to fuck with me. I'm going to be taking over the building, the money, and his fucking life as soon as this is over. And when it's over, it's going to be my way and not the way of the little shit who thinks he's in charge."

Vaughn waited to be shot. He waited for the gun to go off and him not to be around any longer. When he heard a shuffle, he looked at the doorway and watched as McKnight walked through it. He nearly got up to lock him out when he came back.

"Come on, asshole. We have less than an hour to get to the fucking building and kill the cocksucker."

Vaughn was so happy to be allowed to live; he nearly fell over the stool getting to the door. He was in the limo when he realized that he wasn't armed.

The car was his. He'd know this thing anywhere. It was custom to his needs and wants. The driver, however, was not. So when he was told to slide into the corner and behave, he did so without hesitation. There was a gun hidden between each door and seat, and he was just reaching for it when McKnight spoke to the driver.

"Have you cleaned this?" The driver nodded. "Good because if he comes up with a gun or something else that might get me hurt, then I'm going to feed you your nuts. Then I'm going to kill you. Understood?"

Vaughn had a feeling he was asking him if he understood that he too was going to be a dead man, but said nothing. What would have been the point? He looked out the window and thought about what the fuck had gotten him here. Drugs and money, or the lack of money he supposed. But it had cost money to start out, money he didn't have. And when he'd been approached by someone saying they could help him out, he'd nearly drooled at the thought of limitless funds. And they had been limitless at first. By the time he'd been nearly sixty million in debt to this man, he now knew, he was beyond ever paying any of it back. And from the looks of things he wasn't going to have to.

The ride to the building took just under twenty minutes. There was only one vehicle in front of it, and the gates were open. There was no sign of the dogs Mary had told him about, nor were there any guards. He wondered now if there had been either and decided that it mattered little. They each got out of the car, and his driver was told to stay behind.

"'Kay, boss." The man looked like he ate a cow, the entire beast, for lunch. "Be right here for you."

Chapter 17

Curtis looked around the room again. He'd been told where to stand and not to move. The little microphone in his ear bothered him, but not too much. Every time someone spoke to him, he nearly jumped out of his skin. He was getting used to it now because someone had started playing music softly so he wouldn't be startled again. He looked out the window when he heard a car pull in.

"He's here. It looks like there is one in the front seat and one…no, make that two in the back. Are you doing okay, Curtis?"

Curtis nodded at Mann, forgetting that he couldn't see him. But the others could, all ten of the Special Forces that were hiding around inside the building.

"Two? Who else is with him?" Curtis stepped away from the window and leaned against the nearest printer. "Should I be worried?"

"No. We've got you covered from head to toe. And you were right about Kylie. She's now under lock and key. She nearly slipped past one of my men in an attempt to go to you." Curtis smiled at the man's frustrated voice. "She's a little spitfire, isn't she? She took out two of my men before she was subdued."

"Just so you know." Curtis stood when he heard the door below him open. "You hurt her, and I will rip you apart limb by limb and then piss on your dying body."

The two men walked through the doorway just as he heard Mann sputtering. Curtis didn't get mad often, but when someone fucked with what was his, then all bets were off. And he was as serious as it came when it came to Kylie. "You were to come alone. This is not a fucking tea party." The smaller man stopped, and the larger man, one that Curtis knew immediately was in charge, bumped into him. "If you have business with LaMancusa, then you do it on your own time."

The man laughed and knocked LaMancusa out of his way. There was something cold and calculating about this man. He was a killer, and Curtis felt sweat trickle down his spine.

"Oh, you can conduct your business with him. I'm going to be here as a…let's; just call me a casual observer. Continue as if I'm not even here."

Curtis was doubtful that was possible even if LaMancusa didn't look like he was terrified. "And you would be?" Curtis didn't think he'd answer him and was surprised when he did. But the cursing in his ear didn't make him feel any better about the introduction.

"I'm Lambert McKnight. Have you ever heard of me?"

Curtis shook his head and tried his best to ignore the voice in his head.

"I thought not. You're much too straight-laced to have been in my circles."

"He's one of the biggest mob bosses ever to come to this part of the country. Hell, probably the world. He's been connected to more crimes than Capone ever was."

Great news, thought Curtis. *Now fucking what?*

"Don't piss him off."

Curtis thought right then and there that he was going to shoot Mann. The man and his helpful advice, notwithstanding, Curtis wasn't happy with him. Trying to calm his pounding heart, Curtis leaned against the press and smiled. "But my business is with him." He nodded toward LaMancusa. "Him, I know, you not so much."

"Are you fucking trying to get yourself killed?"

Tempted to take the bud out of his ear, Curtis tried once again to ignore him.

"I said *not* to piss him off, not to *try* and piss him off."

"True. You don't. But we can fix that. How would you like to be rich beyond your wildest dreams? How would you like to have more women and more places to go than anyone you know?"

Curtis shrugged.

"Oh come now, Hunter, you have to have more aspirations than simply being a flunky for your older brother?"

"No. I love my family, and I have more money than I can spend right now. And in a few weeks, I'll have more women than I can handle. My lovely wife. I'll have a great deal more when I open that wall up and see what's inside." Curtis didn't look at the place where the money was hidden. "I could simply take what is rightfully mine or split it with that moron and still have what I—"

"*Hey.*" LaMancusa finally spoke up. "That's not very nice, and the deal was that I would let you live, and you'd give me what is rightfully mine."

Curtis looked at the man. He was stupid if he thought that he was coming out of this with anything more than he had in his pockets right now. And when he glanced at McKnight he thought LaMancusa would more than likely not make it out of this building.

"As I have said to you countless times, the money does not belong to you. You can try and take it, but I can tell you right now that I will hunt you down and take more from you than you took from me." Curtis stood straighter and stretched. "I'm tired of this shit. We end this right now."

Before he could move toward the door or to even say the word that would bring the cavalry running, McKnight agreed with him. "Right you are, Hunter. Right you are."

The gun was out and pointed at him. Curtis froze for a few scant seconds then the gun was pointed at LaMancusa. The report of the weapon going off nearly had him cry out, but he was too scared to move.

"What happened? Curtis? Tell me to come in. Mother fuck, he's been shot. I need—"

Curtis spoke before Mann could give the men around him the all clear to come out. "You killed LaMancusa. Why?"

"That's just fucking great. He killed a man right in front of you. Give me the okay to come in. We have enough now to put him away for a few years. Not as much as I'd like, but—"

"I have my reasons. Now it's just you and me. And whoever else you have in this building." Curtis didn't move. "Oh, I'm not nearly as stupid as the man I just killed. And you'd be stupid to come here without support or back up. But you have to know that you'll be a dead man before they can come here, and my man downstairs will get me out before I ever make it to any jail."

"I'm listening." Curtis hoped that Mann was as well. Curtis wasn't quite ready to die just yet. "The money is all yours if there is any."

"There is. I've been doing research as well." McKnight looked at the wall. "You know it as well. Billy Trust wasn't the only person in the FBI building that has loyalties elsewhere."

"Christ. Who? See if you can get him to tell you."

No shit, Curtis wanted to shout at the Fed.

"See if you can get him to at least hint."

Curtis said the first name that popped into his head. "Pamela Long, the agent that first came to us."

He saw the surprise first, then the anger. It flared fast and hot. Curtis waited for the bullet to rip through him. And was very happy when it did not.

"She told you. Not that it matters really, but she has outlived her usefulness. Actually, she did that before I went to visit little Vaughny here. She wanted…she wanted more from our relationship than I wanted her to have. She currently lives in a shallow grave somewhere." McKnight looked around as if he just realized what he'd said. His next words confirmed it. "I suppose there are ears here. Oh well, you'll never testify, and I'll be living in the lap of luxury long before they can sort through this mess."

McKnight walked to the wall that had been put back up. Curtis could see where the new bricks had been brought in and replaced the broken ones, but obviously, McKnight didn't. He went about ten feet from where the damage had been done and looked at Curtis. "Come now, you don't expect them to wait all day on you, do you? You have to have me trying to leave with the money if the charges are going to be big enough to keep me locked away for years and years. I have to be seen leaving with the money. Your death and this shit here isn't going to be enough, and it'll only serve to piss me off more." He pointed the gun at Curtis' head and told him to pick up the sledgehammer.

"No." Curtis wasn't going to help. He was sure he'd be dead, but he wasn't helping. "You want it, then you fucking take it. No sweat off my balls."

The first man to enter the room pointed the gun to McKnight's head. He only smiled. He didn't fight the man, nor did he say anything when he was shoved against the wall and held there. There was something wrong. Very wrong. As the room filled with men in flack vests and armor, Curtis had a feeling, he was missing something. And McKnight's laughter was getting on his last nerve.

"You might want to ask your family where your future father-in-law is. He has been with me for some time now, and he's not going to be found in time if you don't let me go."

Curtis moved toward him and pushed the Special Forces officer out of his way.

"Tisk, tisk now, Hunter, you're letting your temper get the better of you."

"Where is he? You tell me right now or so help me. I'll kill you myself."

The man laughed again. "You won't because your little wifey would never forgive you." McKnight looked over his shoulder, and Curtis knew that someone else had entered the room. "Well, as I live and breathe. If it isn't my old pal Charlie Mann. How is the family?"

Curtis looked at Mann then back at McKnight. The two men stared at each other for several seconds before McKnight was taken away. Curtis turned to Mann and asked him where Jon was.

"We're looking. He was supposed to be at the doctor's office an hour ago, and I had a team there on the outside. As soon as McKnight claimed he had him, I had them go in there. The entire office staff, including the doctor, is dead.

Washington is gone."

"And Kylie? Does she know?" Mann shook his head. "Christ, we have to find him now. He's not well."

"I've got my best men working on it. Like I said, his appointment was an hour ago, so he wouldn't have gotten far. We're doing everything we can to find him."

Curtis knew that he was. But it didn't lessen the fact that he was still missing. As soon as his family arrived, he took Kylie aside and told her. She didn't believe him at first.

"I just spoke to him. He said he was in the office and that he was waiting on the doctor to come in and see him." She looked at him with tears in her eyes. "How did they let this happen to him?"

"I don't know, honey. I have no idea." He held her in his arms and tried to think. He wondered if Jon might already be dead, but didn't say that to Kylie.

~~~

Jon looked around his cell. He knew that he was here because of that LaMancusa person. He tried to think how he'd ended up here and decided that the pain in his head was too much for him to think on that overly hard right now. Jon knew that his arm was broken, as was his hip. The way that man had tossed him into the trunk and slammed the lid shut, it was small wonder that he didn't have more broken bones. He wiped at the tears that seemed to flow down his cheeks. He was going to die.

Jon wasn't an overly brave man. But he wasn't stupid either. He was insurance, plain and simple. LaMancusa wanted to make sure that things went his way, and Jon had been his insurance policy in keeping them all in line. He hoped that they wouldn't worry about one little old man and take the man out, but he knew the heart of the Hunters and knew that they'd never leave him behind. He smiled when he thought of how happy his little girl was going to be as soon as she married young Curtis.

Sitting up off the cold floor, Jon moaned. His hip hurt him so badly that he wasn't sure how long he'd be able to hold in that position. Not long, he figured and tried to see if he could see if anyone was at the doorway again.

"Hello. I was wondering if I might have a pain reliever? I've been hurt badly, and I would very much like something to help me."

"You're not gonna be around long enough to care about a little pain in your old stinking body. Shut the fuck up and sit still. I have a game on, and you're fucking with my entertainment."

Well, Jon thought, *that settles that.* He tried to think of anything but the pain and had to lie back down. His bladder was full, but just thinking about trying to stand to urinate was too much. Closing his eyes, he thought of his only child.

Kylie hadn't been a problem child. Not even for him. She'd been born so late in his life that he'd been terrified of messing her up. He knew nothing of children, being an only child himself, and knew less of little girls. His wife had been so good and kind to him that when she'd passed when Kylie had been a baby, he'd actually thought of putting her up for adoption. But the night he'd come to that very decision and walked into her room to see her one last time had knocked that idea right out of his head.

She'd been awake and not making a sound. When he looked into her bed, she turned her head slightly and stared up at him. She looked at him with her mother's eyes, and she seemed to be telling him that she'd be no trouble for him, that he should give her a chance. He reached down and touched her downy face, and she grabbed his finger.

Love. He'd loved her before that. Loved her with all of his heart and then some, but when she'd touched him, held his finger, his heart had nearly exploded with newfound love. Jon knew in that moment that he would give his all to seeing her grow up, give his life to make her happy, and he'd do anything in the world to keep her safe.

The rattling at the door had him look up. The man standing there held a tray in his hand. Jon knew it was his meal. The same man had been bringing him food since yesterday on the same tray. This time was different only in that Jon didn't have the strength to sit up and eat today.

"Get up."

Jon didn't move. Couldn't move.

"I said to get up and eat. I ain't gonna feed you this shit."

"I have to use the facilities, and I hurt too badly to get myself there. You'll have to help me." The man snorted. "Please. I have hurt my hip, and I need to get up."

The man tossed the tray on the floor. Then he ground his boot into the mess he'd made. As he moved back to the doorway, Jon thought he was going to leave him there. But before he went through it and shut it, he turned back to him. "You eat what's there or nothing. And I'm not your maid, fancy man. You have to piss, then you either get up and do it, or you wet yourself. And I'm not gonna change your pants either. You're on your own."

The door slammed shut, and Jon continued to lay there. He knew now that he was going to die for sure and wished that he could see his lovely daughter once more before he did. Closing his eyes again, he sent up a little prayer. He rarely did that anymore, not since his wife had died, but he did now.

"Please watch over my baby. Please keep her safe and

happy, Lord." He looked at the food in front of him and felt his bladder let go; there was no hope for it. "Lord, I ask you for this in the name of your son. Please make sure that the man who did this to us is held accountable for all that he has done."

Jon moved again; this time, he screamed out in pain. As blackness took him, he remembered Curtis' promise. He'd said he'd keep her safe. Smiling even as he blacked out, his last thought was that the man was going to pay when Curtis found him.

The next time he woke, he was freezing. Jon could see very little. He wasn't sure if the room was dark from the lack of light or that he couldn't see. He found that he didn't care. Pain racked his body relentlessly now, and he cried from it. The man had come in to get the tray, he could see, but the food still lay there. Closing his eyes again, Jon knew in his heart that he'd never open them again. Looking up, he saw his wife and smiled at her.

"Hello, my love."

She nodded at him and held out her hand.

"I can't leave her just yet. She's not safe."

She nodded again and stepped toward him. Jon knew that as soon as he touched her that he'd be pain free and he could move again. He was tempted. Wanted to join her so badly, but there was their little girl to care for.

"She is going to be fine, love. Her man will keep her safe, and the grandchildren she has for us will give us something to watch from where we're going. She is going to be fine, trust me."

Jon nodded now, touched the tip of her fingers, and felt himself being lifted. His body, for the first time in so long, even before he'd been hurt, felt new, revitalized, and almost young again. When he wrapped his hand around his wife's waist and held her, she told him not to look back, that Curtis would take care that he was found. As he moved out of the building, he didn't look at anything but her eyes, the eyes of his child, and knew that she was right; Kylie would be all right from now on.

"I love you so much, Olivia. I've missed you more and more every day." She kissed him, and he held her. "I tried too hard to be a good father. I'm afraid that—"

"You gave her everything she needed. She loved us both because you told her about me."

Jon felt tears spill from his eyes.

"Don't cry, Jon. We can spend our days looking down on her and the children and be happy together once again."

Jon nodded, and, suddenly, he was high above the earth. Settling down on a chair, he watched as Olivia pointed to something beyond them. Looking out, he could see them, all the small children. And he knew these children were going to be babies soon. And a few of them were going to be his. Jon leaned back in his chair, and his lovely wife sat with him. Jon knew that his daughter would be sad for a time, but she would be happy, happier than she'd ever been. Smiling, he held on and closed his eyes. Life had never been sweeter.

Chapter 18

Kylie watched the men move into the house. They had been watching it for a few days, and she simply wanted to go in and find her daddy. He'd been missing for three days now, and she didn't want to think about what might be inside. She reached for and found Curtis' hand and held on tight. Kasey was on her other side, and she, too, held her hand.

"It's going to be all right. We'll go inside, and he'll be sitting in a chair wondering what all the fuss is about." Even to her own ears, she sounded insincere. "We'll be hearing about this for years to come."

Curtis squeezed her hand and said nothing. He knew too, she realized. Knew that her daddy wouldn't be found alive.

The cop had said that the blood they'd found in the trunk of the limo had been more than one person could lose. Her daddy had been hurt along with all those people in that office that day. He'd been taken away for insurance, they'd told her. They'd also told her that the likelihood of them finding him after all this time was nearly impossible.

McKnight wasn't talking. He'd said not a single word other than "no comment" since they'd brought him to the jail.

Now he was sitting in a prison cell waiting on his trial. A trial that Jesse had told her would only be a short time for all they thought he'd done. All they had him on now was the murder of another bad guy, Vaughn LaMancusa.

"It's clear," the man in front of her said.

"Kylie?"

She looked up in the face of someone she knew she should know, but couldn't place. It took her several seconds to realize that it was Annamarie.

"He's dead, isn't he?"

Annemarie nodded.

"Can I see him now? I'd like to see my daddy now, please."

"Not yet, sweetheart. The police..." She wiped at tears that flooded her face. "The police have to make sure that they gather all the evidence. They said that they should be finished soon."

There was a look shared between her and Curtis, and she could almost hear them speaking. She couldn't hear what they were saying but knew that a great deal of information had passed between them before Annamarie walked away. Curtis stepped in front of her.

"Are you sure you want to do this?"

No, she wanted to scream at him. *Hell no.* She looked at him as he continued.

"I can go and look to make sure it's him for you."

"I have to be sure." She trusted him, but she also needed to make one hundred percent sure for herself. "What if he... what if you make a mistake? He might be still out there."

Curtis nodded and pulled her into his arms. "I understand. I had to be sure when my dad died, as well. It was hard not knowing for sure."

They stood like that, in each other's arms, for another hour. Neither of them spoke to each other, but Curtis would answer questions if someone came up to them. She simply let the world go on around her. Her daddy was gone.

When the call came that she could go inside, she hesitated. She looked at Curtis when he stopped with her. He didn't ask her again, though a part of her wished he would. When she took a step back, he nodded once and went to the doorway. Kasey was suddenly there with her.

"He'll do what's right. He loves you too much not to."

Kylie nodded.

"When my mother passed away, the Hunters were so great. My world had ended when she did. Curtis and the rest of them were so supportive then." She grinned at her. "Not so much, Royce. He was a royal pain in the ass, but I still love him."

"You and Royce didn't always love each other?" Kylie let her distract her. "I thought the two of you had been in love since birth."

Kasey laughed. "Hardly. He was an overbearing, irritating asshole. Come to think of it, he still is. There are days when I want to wring his neck. Other days, I want to crawl up into his heart and stay there."

"You already are there, love." Royce reached out and pulled Kasey into his arms. "And I heard you describe me as a pain in your ass. You do know that you're no picnic either."

They both laughed, as did Kylie. She was still smiling when Curtis came out with a gurney. There was a bag on it, closed and strapped down. She started to step toward it and him when Royce pulled her back.

Curtis came to her then and simply held her. "He's been gone for a few days. The coroner thinks he had a heart attack.

He'd been hurt too and had lost a good deal of blood." He pulled her back and looked into her face. "It was Jon. I swear to you, Kylie, it was your dad."

The tears came then. Hard and hot. She couldn't have stopped them even if she had tried. She felt herself being lifted up and moved but didn't care. When she was closed up in the back of the SUV that she'd been brought over in, she curled up in the seat and cried harder. Her daddy was gone. The door on the other side opened, and she knew it was Curtis. He started the engine, and they were moving before she could ask him where they were going. She looked up at the house that he stopped in front of. Curtis began speaking before she could say anything.

"He was lying on the cold floor when I walked in. There was food in front of him that had been there for a while, as well. His body...I think his hip was broken, as was his arm. That's where the blood had come from, his arm." He blew his nose twice before continuing, and she realized he'd been crying too. "They left that man there to die. He'd wet himself. They didn't even have the good manners to help him to the toilet."

"Daddy would have hated people knowing that he'd done that. He had so much pride in himself."

Curtis nodded.

"Do you think he suffered much?"

He looked at her then out the window again. "I don't know, honey. But I have to tell you something. I don't know if you'll believe me or not, but I'm going to tell you anyway. He was smiling."

She sat up in the chair and looked at him. When she said his name, he looked at her. "What do you mean, smiling? You think he was happy he was dying?" Curtis was shaking his head before she finished. "Then what?"

"I think he was happy because..." He looked right at her this time, and she could see that he was very serious. "He looked like he was happy because he saw something or someone he loved."

Kylie looked out the window, trying to figure that out. Someone he loved? She was all he had. Then it occurred to her. She looked at Curtis. "My mother. She was there with him. You think that, don't you?" He nodded. "You think that my mom came to...to collect him when he passed over, and he was happy to see her."

"Yes, I do."

Kylie looked out the window again. The rain was coming down softly on the windshield, and the wipers were moving just as gently. Her mother. Her daddy had always told her when his time came, he was going to be happy to see his Olivia. He had told her for years that she would be there to take him to heaven, and he'd go with her willingly.

"I won't lie to you, Kylie. Not ever and not about something as important to you as this. Your father looked happy." He reached into his coat pocket and held his hand out to her. "They gave me this so that I could give it to you."

Kylie held out her hand and felt the cold chain tumble into her palm. She knew what it was as soon as she curled her fingers around it. Opening her fingers, she looked at the locket and chain her father had worn around his neck her entire life.

Opening it, she heard the tinny sound of the chimes and listened to them for a minute as she looked at the pictures of her parents on their wedding day. Both of them so very happy-looking and so full of hope. She ran her fingers over their likeness before closing it back up. It was a beautiful piece. One she'd seen her mother wear when Kylie was just a child. The work on it, the hearts that encircled, reminded her of her parents so much. She leaned her head on the back of the seat and looked at Curtis.

"It was my mom's. Daddy wore it all the time after she died. He told me once that it was his lifeline to her. That so long as he wore it, she'd be near him. He said that the only time he was ever going to remove it was when she came to get him." She slipped it over her head and looked down at it. "I believe you. My mom came to get him and to end his suffering. I can…I can move on knowing that he's in a much better place and he's with her. Daddy loved my mom very much."

Curtis nodded. "And I love you. Very much."

~~~

The house was empty now of police and medics. They'd uncovered five bodies so far in the yard and the land beyond the pool. The house was now filled with Hunters. His family and the Federal agent that had gotten them this far, Charles Mann. He looked over at the camera crew that was recording this so that if anything found in the safe was used in a court of law, they had proof of where it had originated from. Curtis looked at Jesse when he cleared his throat.

"We can't see what's in the sucker if you don't open it. You do have the combinations still, right?"

Curtis nodded. "Well, what the heck are you waiting for?"

"I don't know." He didn't either. "What if there's nothing inside? What if this whole thing was something she concocted to get what she wanted?"

Michelle LaMancusa had been freed from protective custody. It was at her request. And since she'd been so helpful in getting them where they were now, in front of a safe that hadn't been opened in nearly thirty years, they gave her what she wanted.

"She has her life back now. She's signed over all rights to the house and its contents to you. There isn't anything in this house she said she wanted." Jesse leaned down on his knees. "Open the safe so we can all go home. If it's empty, then so what? If it has half of what she claims is in it, then McKnight is going away for a very long time."

McKnight was still in jail and awaiting a trial. They, the Feds, had tried their best to get him to talk, but all he did was smile and nod at them. He'd told them that he'd had no idea that Jon Washington was inside the home of LaMancusa and that he'd thought the man unstable. That was the reason he'd shot him that day so that he wouldn't harm Curtis.

Neither Curtis nor anyone else believed him. But without something, he was going to spend only five years in prison and then be out again. And it could all very well be right here, all the information that they needed to put him away for a very long time if what Michelle had told them was true. He pulled out the small piece of paper and turned the dial to the first number.

There were eight numbers. All of them had to be hit precisely, or the safe wouldn't open. Michelle had told him and Kylie that the numbers lined up perfectly for "Michelle." Each number was a letter of the alphabet that spelled out her name. He turned to the first number thirteen. He'd had to stop once to wipe the sweat off his hands and the second time to try and remember how to make sure the numbers were correct. The sound of the final number falling into place was loud in the room.

He was supposed to step back and let the professionals open the safe. He simply couldn't do it. Curtis needed to see that all this hadn't been for nothing. When he put his hand on the handle, he half expected someone to tackle him out of the way. When no one did, he turned it downward and pulled hard.

At first, there was nothing he could see. The thing was huge anyway and set back in a large breakaway wall. Someone had gone to a great deal of trouble to put the safe where no one would see it, and they hadn't bothered with much in the way of lighting. A light was suddenly shining over his shoulder and into the darkened space. He never turned to thank whoever it was because what was in there caught his full attention.

"Mother of God." His brother Royce, he'd know that voice anywhere. "He could have lived like a god with all of that."

There were stacks of money along the right side of the wall. Since the exterior was nearly six feet, Curtis figured that the interior was about four and a half. And the money was from the bottom to the top. Reaching in slowly, he was stopped when someone shoved a pair of latex gloves at him. The word "fingerprints" made him pull them on.

The topmost stack was of hundreds. Curtis knew that each bank bundle would hold one hundred of the money it bound. So this stack of hundreds was ten thousand dollars. Pulling them out one at a time, he counted fifty of them. It was confirmed by the man behind him. The next fifty stacks of fifty dollar bills. He expected ones to be next but was surprised by the picture of Grover Cleveland. There were nearly two hundred stacks of these, one hundred and ninety-eight to be precise.

But that wasn't all that was inside the safe. There were five large metal boxes in there as well. There were no locks on them, probably because they were locked in the safe. Curtis didn't open them but handed them back to the man collecting them. The notebooks, six of them, was what he wanted.

The oldest one was dated nearly fifty years ago. He only skimmed over it and handed it back. The next two, he did the same. As he looked over the next one, he saw names he'd read about. Men who were reputed to be in the mob. Men and women who had been killed and had killed. It wasn't until the last two that he saw a name he'd been looking for.

"He's in here. McKnight. He's right here." He handed the fifth volume to Mann and continued to look at the last one. "And here. He's all over this one."

Mann took the book with latex-covered hands. He smiled when he'd only read a few pages, and Curtis knew that it had what he'd wanted. At least, he figured, enough to hold the man for a lot longer than they had first feared.

Mann pulled out his cell and walked away, talking into it as Curtis looked at his brothers. "I guess it's over."

"Not quite." Jesse smiled. "I've been doing a bit of my own work. I'm sure you won't mind, but I wanted to make sure that you were covered, as well as Kylie. I've made a few deals. Deals that I hope you share with the company."

Curtis frowned at him. "What have you been up to?"

When Curtis left the house, he was still reeling. His brother had been a very busy boy. And now he had to go and tell Kylie. He just hoped that she was as understanding…half as understanding as he'd been. Christ, he hoped she was.

She was in the kitchen when he came into the house. The decorators had been there, he could see. Several cabinets had yet to be placed, but their new refrigerator was installed, as well as the windows. Kylie was sitting in the breakfast nook reading something. He watched her for several minutes before she looked up.

"Hi. I was just reading over our first article from the paper. It's pretty good. I only found three mistakes so far."

He nodded at her and went to sit beside her.

"The new program does well with spell check, but it matters little if it's not the correct word."

"There are times when I wish I had something to tell me when I use the incorrect word. You've no idea how many times I get to a business meeting and realize that instead of putting 'your' I should have used 'you're.'" Curtis leaned back in the chair and tried to think of what to tell her and how.

"Your brother called. He said that you and he had a long meeting. That I wasn't to think you were having a torrid affair with some woman." She smiled. "I told him that I knew you weren't. I said that I keep you pretty well worn out."

Curtis laughed. It was sudden and loud. She'd caught him off guard once again with her wit and humor. He took her hand and kissed it. "The notebooks were right where Michelle said they'd be. All of them, including the primer." He pulled out the small piece of paper that Jesse had given him. "This is an accounting of what they figured out in the hour they looked them over. Mostly we looked over the later ones, and it looks like McKnight is going away for a very long time."

She got up and poured him a glass of tea and handed him a cookie jar. He opened it to find not only his favorite chocolate chip but caramel crunch too. He ate one as she sat down and took one herself.

"You'll feel a lot better if you just tell me, Curtis. This beating around the bush is annoying and time consuming. Just tell me." She put her cookie down. "There was nothing there, but the books wasn't there?"

He nodded, then shook his head. "There were several

boxes of jewels. From the first look, there was nothing on the list that they had, so most of that will be ours. I tried to contact Michelle to let her know what was there, and she said she didn't care. She told me again that whatever is there, I could do whatever I wanted with it." She nodded as he continued. "The bags at the Washington building have been taken. As of five o'clock, the building is a crime scene. Jesse made a deal with the Feds on what happens to that." He got up to pace and talk. "The money is going to go to the insurance company. All of it. The company said that there would be a reward, but he didn't know how long it would take before the company finalized it, so it might be awhile. The reward will be about fifty thousand."

"That's a tidy sum."

He looked at her to see if she was kidding, and he knew that she wasn't. Her voice seemed relieved. Curtis sat back down. "There was money in the safe at the house. According to the claim made by Jesse on our behalf, we get that all the entire amount. And the jewels that no one claims." She nodded at him. "There's more than anyone thought."

"So will it be enough to fund the building? Will we have to borrow to bring it up to code? I know that you said you have the funds, but I'd really like to make this happen with donations and money from all this. My dad would have liked that."

He nodded again and smiled.

"So, there's enough?"

"I think there will be plenty. In addition to the money and jewels, we get the bearer bonds as well. Some of them that Jesse has had a chance to look at will be enough to do whatever we want."

She looked confused. Kylie opened her mouth twice to

say something then closed it. When she finally spoke, he nearly burst out laughing. She was going to kill him.

"So just how much was there? You know I hope you're not like this at Christmas. I hate all the secrecy."

Chapter 19

The building was set to unveil in the morning. Kylie couldn't sleep. And every time she rolled over, Curtis would pull her back into his arms and snuggle into her. She was too tense to enjoy him, so she got up. Going to the kitchen to make herself a cup of tea, she realized that the unveiling was today in about four hours, not tomorrow.

The phone ringing startled her, and she picked up the receiver with a shaky hand. "Oh good," Annamarie said in the way of greeting. "I was afraid you'd be asleep, and I wanted to talk to you."

"This is Kylie, Annamarie. If you want Curtis, I can go and wake him up for you. I couldn't sleep. Nerves, I guess." She realized she was babbling and snapped her mouth closed.

"I was calling you, dear. I knew that he wouldn't be awake. I've never seen a boy that, when he was tired, could sleep through a bomb going off. No, I hoped to speak to you. What are you calling the building?"

They'd been going around about this for several weeks. It started at her father's funeral and had been an ongoing question since then. Kylie smiled. She hadn't told anyone what the name was going to be, not even Curtis. "The name will be revealed today. Are you going to be there?" Kylie giggled when Annamarie cursed. "What would your sons say if they heard you right now?"

"They'd not say a word if they knew what was good for them. Why won't you tell me? I tried to bribe that young man at the printer shop and all he told me was that you wouldn't pay for his college if he told. That's terribly unfair of you, young lady." She huffed. "If you've named it something ridiculous, then I'm not ever going to speak to you again."

Kylie smiled and didn't say a word. After a minute or two, Annamarie huffed again. "I've never met a more stubborn girl in my life."

"I'm sure you have. Have you peeked in the mirror today?" Kylie laughed harder. She hadn't realized how much she needed this. "Annamarie, I promise you that you and the others won't be disappointed. I've given a great deal of thought to this building, and I want it to be a success."

As they were leaving the house, she looked at Curtis, suddenly nervous. Today was the big day. She stopped right outside the car and took several deep breaths. He came around the car and held her.

"You'll do fine. I swear to you that no one will laugh at you." She glared at him. "I'm kidding, love. You're going to be fine like I said. And when this is over, I'm going to bring you back here and break in our new mattress."

Kylie snorted. "We broke it in five times already. Twice last night. If ever a mattress was broken in, you did it." She took another deep breath. "All that money."

Over forty million dollars had been what they had ended up with. That didn't even include the jewels. She looked down at the ring he'd given her yesterday and watched it sparkle off the sunlight.

"All that and more. And the way it's working for the building, downtown will help a great many people. You should be very proud of yourself."

She was, but no less nervous. When he pulled her back and kissed her, she slipped into the car and buckled in. It was time. She had to face those people, her new family included, and see if they would accept her.

There were nearly twice as many people as there were chairs. And because of that, they moved everything to the outside. The parking lot was filled with cars, people, and news crews. She looked at Curtis when he came to sit beside her.

"You should know that someone put several buckets for extra donations around the parking lot. And whoever it was put an armed guard at each one. Last I heard, they'd had to replace them all at least three times. It's going to be well funded from now on."

She nodded. The money that they'd used to renovate the building had come from the money that had been what had gotten her father killed. They had hoped that donations, as well as grants, would keep it up from now on. When it was her turn to stand up and speak, she nearly tripped over the wires running along the floor. She smiled at the people when she looked out over the crowd.

"My father once told me that you can get more people to listen to you if you simply get to the point. That's the way he ran his paper and his life. So if you all will give me just one minute, I'll get to the unveiling." She turned to the man at the ropes and nodded. He yanked once then twice before he had to get on a ladder to see if the sheet would come down that way. She turned back to the crowd. "He didn't say it would be easy, he just said to get to the point."

There was a great deal of laughter. She turned back in time to see the large sheet slip from the sign. It was more beautiful than she'd imagined it would be. She stepped back up to the microphone and smiled as she brushed away the tears.

"This building is named for two remarkable men. One of them was my father, Jon Philip Washington, and for Royce Daniel Hunter, my future husband's father. Both men gave their lives for something they believed in. What, you ask? They gave it for love." She turned back to the building as she continued. "And this is their love back to you. Please welcome the first of many educational mentorships for teenagers, The Hunter Washington Guidance Center."

She stepped away from the microphone and toward Curtis. It wasn't until she was in his arms that she realized people were clapping. Curtis led her back to the mike and held her hand above her head. They loved it. They loved the building.

By the time the reception was over, she was exhausted. Curtis had stayed beside her all night, and when she'd yawned for the tenth time in as many minutes, he picked her up and took her to the car. She was nearly asleep when she felt the seat under her. By the time they were home, she knew that he'd taken her shoes off and her stockings. She was beyond caring. Yawning again, she rolled over in the bed as soon as she was in it and closed her eyes. Not a single thought entered her head as she tumbled into a deep sleep.

~~~

Curtis wanted to wake her but knew that she had been so tired the night before that he kept telling himself she needed this. What he really wanted to do was to wake her with his mouth, but wasn't sure she'd be receptive of that yet. Smiling, he thought about learning all sorts of things about his future wife. If she ever woke up. Finally, at ten-thirty, he kissed her shoulder.

"Babe. You have to get up. We have to leave here soon." She growled at him and rolled over. "If you don't get up, I'm going to take you and put you in the shower myself."

"Go 'way. Tired."

He grinned again.

"Tired."

"I know, honey, but the limo is going to be here in forty-five minutes, and you're not dressed yet." She didn't stir, so he kissed her again. "You did remember that we're getting married today, right?"

Her head came up so quickly that she caught him in the chin. If he hadn't been moving back, she might have made him bite his tongue. As it was, he only saw a few stars. She tossed the covers off and hopped out of bed so quickly that he'd not had time to get to steal a small kiss from her.

"Why didn't you wake me up? Damn it, Curtis, we're supposed to meet your mom at the courthouse early. What's she going to think if we show up late?" She was tossing things around the room. "Where is my dress?"

He pointed to the closet, glad now that he'd set every clock in this room two hours ahead. He watched as she took out the dress she'd picked out and laid it across the bed. When she went to the shower, he waited until the water turned on before he stood up and stripped down. He was going to wash her back. And anything else she'd let him.

The water was steaming up the mirror when he walked in. Sliding back the door, he stepped in behind her just as she was pulling the bottle of shampoo off the shelf. He took the bottle from her as he turned her in his arms.

Her mouth was hot. Trying to set the bottle back on the shelf as he pressed her to the wall, he heard it hit the tile floor and forgot about it. He had a lot more things in mind than showering.

"We don't have time for this." He kissed her again to shut her up. But she pulled her head back. "Curtis, seriously, we have to hurry."

"I gave us plenty of time. I know how you are about getting somewhere on time. I set the clocks ahead for us." He lowered his head to her nipple and took the tip into his mouth. "Hum, just what I needed to start my day."

"I should be upset with—oh yes, Curtis, again."

He slid his finger into her heat and pinched her clit.

"Please make me come."

"Not yet. I want to drink from you when you do." Dropping to his knees, he turned her so that she could sit on the seat in the stall. "You should know that it was my plan to do this last night, but you were sleeping so soundly that I couldn't wake you."

"Less talking and more sex." She leaned back and looked at him through hooded eyes. "Please."

He opened her thighs wider and kissed her gently. He pulled her forward on the bench seat until she was on the very edge. Water slid down his back, and he wondered how much hotter it had gotten since they'd entered here.

Lowering his head, he slid his fingers into her again. She was wet and hot, tight, and hard. Suckling her clit, he brought her to her first of what he hoped was many quick climaxes this morning.

Her nectar was sweet and spicy, and he lapped greedily at her. When she started to rise up to try and get more from him, he pulled her closer to him and ate at her. Christ, she was coming around his tongue. The more he ate at her clit and pussy, the wetter she became, and her climaxes were getting stronger as well.

Standing up, she reached for him. Licking her lips, she wrapped her hand around him, and he nearly let her take him into her mouth. But he needed to be inside of her, and if she even touched him, he was going to go.

Curtis sat on the bench when he stood her up. He noticed she was trembling, and he held her while he positioned himself. Once he was where he wanted to be Curtis pulled her forward and helped her straddle his lap. Lowering her over his cock, he nearly came when she brushed his mouth with her nipple. Grabbing a mouthful of her flesh, he took as much as he could into him and nipped none too gently at her.

"Please, Curtis. Please?"

He moved her over him more and fisted his cock. Sliding over him, she rode his thick head as he continued to take more of her. By the time she seated herself onto him, he was ready to explode. When she didn't move, he pulled her hips closer to him.

"I love you."

He stopped moving and looked at her. His mind was a blaze of lust.

"I love you very much."

Curtis leaned his forehead onto hers. "I love you as well. I've loved you forever and ever."

She lifted her head. "You should know that if I didn't need you as much as you seemed to need me, I would have kicked your ass for lying to me."

He nodded. "Yes, ma'am. I'll remember that next time." He pulled her hips forward. "Do you think we can finish this before my balls explode?"

She threw back her head, and he took her nipple again. Standing, he pressed her against the tile wall and took her as gently as he could. Slow, even strokes filled her and gave him such incredible pleasure that he thought he could do this all day. When she nipped at his earlobe, Curtis cried out and came.

There had been no warning from his body, only that sensation seconds before he came. He was still rocking into her sheath when she came with a scream. Curtis had to stand holding onto the wall for several minutes before he could move. Taking her to the sink, he sat her down and held her. His body was drained. For now.

They were walking in the door to the courthouse when his cell phone went off. He grinned when he saw who it was. Laughing, he answered his mom.

"We're here. Running just a tad behind." He looked over at Kylie and smiled. "Kylie was on time. It was me that was late."

"Get in here now. The judge doesn't have all day." She was laughing and told him she loved him. "Your brothers aren't as patient as I am."

He closed the phone and pulled Kylie into his arms for one more kiss. Then they went to the elevators. She had begged him for a courthouse wedding, and he couldn't help but give her whatever she wanted. But that didn't mean he couldn't make it special.

As soon as the doors slid open, the band started. They began playing the wedding march as they stepped out. His brother Royce took her arm, and Curtis stepped away to move to where the judge, as well as a couple of Kylie's friends and Kasey, stood. Everyone was set.

As Royce brought her to him, both his brothers stood

beside him. Curtis winked at his mom. This was all he could hope for. Especially when he thought of what might have been.

The money they'd found hadn't come easy. There were laws governing it, as well as the jewels. But after postponing the wedding three times, they could no longer wait on the courts to make their decision. They wanted to begin their life as man and wife. Plus, his mom really wanted them wed.

"You happy?"

Curtis glanced at his brother Daniel who he knew had something to do with them being together all along.

"You love her, don't you?"

"Yes." Kylie was only a few steps away when he turned and looked at Daniel. "Why would I be marrying her if I didn't?"

"I was afraid that I'd called your hand."

Curtis looked at him, confused.

"At the dance. I wanted to make you jealous, so…nothing happened between us. I knew then that you loved her."

Kylie stood before him, and he looked at Daniel once more. "I have never loved anyone more in all my life as I do this woman." He hugged his brother before taking Kylie from Royce. "And I love you all as well."

Kylie kissed him and turned to the judge. "Can we get this show on the road before we have a crying fest with the Hunter boys?"

Everyone laughed as they took their places. Curtis leaned over and nipped at her ear. "You're so going to pay for that."

"I certainly hope so. I really do."

About the Author

Hello! My name is Kathi Barton, and I'm an author. I have been married to my very best friend, Sonny, for at times, seems several lifetimes – in a good way, honey. And together, we have three wonderful children and then the ones we brought into the world - Paul and Dale Barton, Jason and Wendy Barton, and Danielle and Ben Conklin. They have given us seven of the greatest treasures on Earth. They don't live at home seven days a week! No, seriously, seven grandchildren – Gavin, Spring, Ben, Trinity, Sarah, Kelly, and Kian.

Follow Kathi on her blog: http://kathisbartonauthor.blogspot.com/

Made in United States
North Haven, CT
02 June 2024